The Wind Could Blow a Bug

The Wind Could Blow a Bug

The Riley Sisters

Book 1

By Jennifer Friess

Mr. Ugly-Man Entertainment
Adrian, Michigan

Mr. Ugly-Man Entertainment
Adrian, Michigan
First Edition December 2014
Text copyright ©2014 by Jennifer Friess
To book an event or to purchase additional copies, please visit:
imnotstalkingyou.com

ISBN 9780692339565

To Elizabeth, who knows the loneliness of college as I do, and who has put up with listening to my silly hopes and dreams for more years than I would care to admit.

Who am I?

I am the girl
who still smiles
and holds back the giggles
when the word "sex"
is said in a class,
letting everyone know
the thoughts that are racing
through my head.
I am the girl
who plays Pole Position
time after time,
driving on the rumble strips every time,
and truly believing I could never do
any better.
I am the girl
who keeps a picture of
James Dean
on my bedroom wall,
though he died years before
I was everborn—
because I like the mystery
of never really knowing him.
--JLF

1

JANE

The Oakley town council meeting had started off typically enough. There was a review of the minutes from the last meeting, and the usual complaints about too much. This time it was too much noise and chickens. But with all the Tucker boys in attendance for the meeting tonight, a rare occurrence, it was only a matter of time before things got rowdy.

The main order of new business on the agenda was to discuss a nationwide pharmacy with plans to build a store at the edge of town. The tiny town, population 3,300, was divided on this particular issue. And so they piled into mayor Skip Wickley's living room for tonight's meeting.

Skip was a large black man, in both mass and stature. He was an impressive physical figure to lead the town, but he was often too busy trying to keep everyone happy to make effective decisions.

On a night of a normal meeting, there would have been plenty of room for everyone. Skip had a large old farmhouse. Usually only 30 or so citizens were in attendance. Tonight it looked as though a representative from almost every household in town was here. The living room and dining room were one combined space, as though a wall that had formerly divided them a hundred years ago had since been removed. Every inch of that space was needed tonight.

Jane Riley sat in the corner on the couch, with her spiral-bound notebook on her lap. Although only a high school senior, she was present at all the town council meetings. She took down notes and turned them into the regional newspaper to earn extra money for college. Twenty dollars per meeting. Since the town council was so small, her newspaper recap also served as official meeting minutes. Being quiet with few hobbies, she would take advantage of that on her college application by saying she was the secretary for the town council. As no one officially held that post, no one could really complain if she claimed it.

But tonight she was too distracted to take conscientious notes. Her attention was not on the debate, but instead on the group of four strapping farm boys standing up, trying to holler over one another. The Tucker boys were not the type of guys to give Jane the time of day. They were all older than Jane. Then again, no other boys in town were interested in her either. Jane had earned a reputation for being "shy", a word she *hated*. In truth, she just didn't care to socialize with the jocks and cheerleaders of her school. They had no clue that she could be funny and witty. Jane saw this as their loss, not hers. She was average in just about every way. She was an average height, with a thin frame, and light brown hair of an average length. She was often mistaken for several years younger than her 18 years. If Jane was a boy, she probably wouldn't be interested in herself either.

The Tucker brothers all had hair damp from the showers they had taken before attending the meeting. It was nice that they had been considerate enough to wash off the day's worth of dirt and sweat before they came. But they also had drowned themselves in cologne too. Were they all heading to the bar to pick up chicks after the meeting? The mix of four different colognes and testosterone filled the room and made Jane's head spin, in a good way.

Evan Tucker was the father of all these men. He was nearing 50. While most fathers were old and chubby and balding, Evan was still a good-looking man. He would look right at home in an Eddie Bauer catalog. His full head of black hair was just starting to have some white mix in around the edges.

Randy was the oldest son. He had to be about 27 now, and helped his father run the business. He looked a lot like his father, but Randy was a few inches taller.

Josh was the second oldest. He was known around town as a prankster. This somehow made him easy to dislike. Josh sported a headful of brown hair and wore a goatee of perpetual stubble on his chin. Jane assumed that he did the same work on the farm as his brothers, but somehow he was thicker around the middle than the rest. He was 24 years old.

Wade was just a year younger than Josh. Wade was the Tucker boy most of the girls in town liked best. He had won the genetics lottery. Blond hair, blue eyes, and a face like a model. His smile had been known to stop traffic.

Oakley's main street only had two lanes and one flashing signal. So really, sometimes a stray cat stopped traffic as well.

Pete was the youngest son. He had been a year ahead of Jane in school, which meant he was now out of school. He looked a lot like his mother. He was wiry, with dirty blond hair.

The discussion was breaking down as everyone talked over each other.

"The SaveRX would bring many jobs to our town."

"But it would put my drug store out of business."

"It sounds like a budget strip club."

"The people from Parker would get all the jobs anyway." This was unlikely. Parker was the next largest town about 40 miles away.

"Wouldn't they need to use some of my land to build it at the proposed site? I am not selling. Does that mean you are going to use eminent domain to claim it?" asked Evan Tucker.

Now it was more obvious why the Tuckers were here. Mr. Tucker owned much of the farmland around Oakley, including all of the farmland on the west end of town where the pharmacy was to be built. He may look like a hick, but he was a very smart businessman. Mr. Tucker had kept his farm going and growing in a time when many had failed. He had managed to keep it in the family as well, an even bigger feat.

Tucker Farms had been started by Evan Tucker's grandfather. Then it was very small and only fed the immediate family. Evan's father grew it to have many cash crops and added many silos for grain storage to cover himself in times of bad weather until his death.

Evan took over the business in very different times. The old-time farmers were dying out, literally, and their children did not want to continue. They wanted to get jobs at the automotive factory in Parker that offered a steady income and benefits. Or they just moved away to the cities, where they could get a job in anything. Evan started buying up the land. Often times he could not offer much, but the sellers snapped it up just to be rid of it. Evan began to diversify his products.

As Evan's business was growing, the local grain elevators, the Oakley Co-Op, just called 'the Co-Op' by locals, were suffering. With the drop in the number of farmers using their buy, sell, and store services, they did not have the ability to make upgrades or pay their employees. When the Co-Op went out of business, Evan was put in the position of expanding his own operation to provide the services to other farmers in and around Oakley that they could no longer receive anywhere else. In a day and age when no one put down new railroad tracks, Evan found he had justification to have some laid between his elevators and the nearest rail spur a few miles away.

Evan had helped salvage what little community was left in Oakley. The goods he bought from the feed store and the hardware store kept them in business. The local tractor supply helped to keep his farming machines in running order. And so on. In turn, all those merchants could buy newspapers, groceries, and eat at the two restaurants in town. It was a delicate balance. Evan Tucker knew this, and it no doubt kept him up late nights.

"Ya, we ain't selling," Josh said.

"That is prime farmland," Randy articulated.

"It is also the best make out spot in town," Wade said, smiling.

"You should know, Wade!" someone in the back yelled.

With that, the room let out a whoop and the conversation quickly was derailed from the task at hand. Wade seemed to be at the center of the chaos.

A great dig at Wade came to Jane. She crossed the room to get closer to the action, waiting for her turn to contribute. She felt self-conscious standing, so she sat in an available chair, left vacant by all those now standing. Wanting a better vantage point of the room, she sat on the back of the stuffed green plaid chair and put her pink Converse shoes on the seat. She began to remember that she wasn't the kind of girl to speak up in meetings, especially to flirt with guys. As the conversation moved away from Wade, Jane knew her chance was gone. This made her relax a little. Although her brief moment of bravery, of just moving across the room, had already made her deodorant fail.

2

The 7:00PM meeting eventually drew to a close around 9:30PM. Jane remained sitting on, not in, the chair, watching everyone mingle as they left. She didn't look forward to going home to her room to listen to music by herself. Jane enjoyed the company of people, as long as she didn't have to actually interact with them.

She glanced out the front picture window. The purple and yellow sunset that had been framed when she had arrived was now like the black of a computer screen, powered down. A steady stream of headlights began passing on the street as people started to depart. Jane looked up at the three diamond shaped windows on the front door. How 1970's, she thought. A new front door would go a long way toward adding value to Skip Wickley's house. Jane touched the corner of the end table next to the chair she sat on, where the wood grain paper was peeling back from the particle board.

"You looked like you were about to say something tonight."

Jane had been so intently studying the worn, low budget furniture that she had not realized anyone had approached. She jumped as she realized the voice came from right in front of her and was directed at her.

"Um, ya. But it was stupid," Jane replied.

Wade Tucker stood in front of her, his face merely inches from hers. His eyes were like two swimming pools of blue, staring back at her.

"Oh, I doubt anything that comes out of your mouth is stupid," Wade said, with a crooked smile.

"How would you know that?" He was starting a conversation with her, and Jane was angry at herself for taking the bait. She felt her cheeks warming.

"It is well known that you are the town smarty-pants," he drawled.

"Oh, ya. Because that is something *great* to be known for." It came out sarcastically. Which is how Jane meant it. But she usually didn't express how she really felt to anyone.

She didn't try to be smart, it just came naturally, like the way her heart was about to jump right out of her chest at this moment in time.

"Naw, it is. Better than being known as the make out king of West Oakley."

"I don't know about that." It slipped out of Jane's mouth before she could sensor it. Her already warm cheeks now burned like a fire.

"Hmmm. Well. . . Now you got me curious." He leaned in closer to Jane. The cologne smell was overpowering. So was his bicep that bulged as he leaned on the arm of the chair right next to her. Jane couldn't help herself from glancing at it, but regretted it when she looked back into his now twinkling blue eyes, realizing she had been caught checking him out.

His blond hair was now dry and a few strands were falling across his forehead. He was so close to her that she could see the freckles on the bridge of his nose. She could feel his breath on her face. She longed to close the tiny distance between the two of them and kiss his lips. All other thoughts had emptied from her mind. Jane was dying to know what it would feel like to have his lips on hers, to suck his lips, to feel his tongue. She had never kissed a boy. He probably wouldn't be the ideal boy to start with, but his confidence and reputation made it very appealing. The reality was if she kissed him right now, he would think she was insane and probably run out the door screaming.

"What were you so eager to add to the discussion tonight?"

Jane inhaled deeply to bring herself back to reality, as best she could anyway.

"Never mind. Nothing important."

"You can tell me."

"Umm. You might get mad."

"A few minutes ago you were ready to say it in front of my friends and family, and now you are afraid it will make me mad?" Wade chuckled.

"Yes."

"It's OK. I want to know."

"I—I was just going to say that if you let them build the SaveRX on your property, then you could just make out in the parking lot, or better yet, in the 'family planning' aisle, and you would never have to worry about running out of protection." Jane was surprised she could push out the joke that had seemed so funny a few minutes earlier. Her voice was a louder volume than she had thought she could manage, although it was shaky and lacked confidence. She looked up now into Wade's burning eyes. He didn't miss a beat.

"Now, Janie Riley, you do surprise me." With that, he smiled and walked away.

The smile that could stop traffic had just made her heart skip a beat.

Jane almost ran out of the room. The cool, humid spring air on her burning skin would be very refreshing on her walk home. Now she couldn't wait to get home and over-analyze every second of her interaction with Wade. She knew she was making a big thing out of a tiny verbal exchange. But that was the closest to actual physical contact she had ever come to with a guy. God, was that depressing to admit at 18, even to herself.

3

The next day after school, Jane went to the post office. As she pushed open the heavy glass door with the brushed silver frame on the right, she saw Mr. Tucker exiting on the left. Her heart jumped a beat. Not only did it make her remember her interaction with his son Wade at the meeting last night, it also made Jane think about the anonymous letter she had mailed to him using a post office box address from this same location last week.

Mr. Tucker,

You are an esteemed business man and do many great things for this community. I was wondering if you could do something for me.

Do you know if your cousin Connie, who lives in Huntington, ever gave up a child for adoption? I might be that baby. I don't want any money from your family. I just want to know where I came from. Respond back to this address.

—Anonymous

P.O. Box 40

Oakley, AL 55555

Jane approached her PO Box. She already had the tiny key in her hand inside the pocket of her gray hoodie. She gave a quick glance around her and opened the door to the box as hurriedly as she could without looking suspicious. She almost squealed when her fingers grasped onto the envelope inside. Jane pulled it out, shoved it into her school bag, and closed the door on the box, all in one swift movement. She almost ran home, wanting to open it as quickly as possible.

Jane Riley had always known she was adopted. How could she not know? Two years after adopting her as a newborn, her parents Stanley and Helen Riley, had been lucky enough to have gotten pregnant when no one thought they could. And with twins! Identical twin girls!

Stanley, "Stan" to his bowling team, was an accountant. And he looked like one. He wore glasses and his hair was getting dangerously close to qualifying as a comb over. He was thick in the middle, so that his chest headed straight into his pants, with no hesitation whatsoever.

Jane knew from pictures that Helen had been quite pretty when she was young, but now she just looked like a mom, a little tired all the time. She wore a constant expression of distraction, as if she was busy trying to remember if there was any milk in the refrigerator. She was thin. This seemed to be more from not having time to eat meals than from trying to consciously live a healthy lifestyle. She worked as a file clerk. Although they both worked, the Rileys were not rich. Jane didn't even have her own car.

To their credit, they didn't send Jane back. But some days she secretly wished that they had. They weren't bad people. She got fed three square meals a day and was never locked in a closet or a dungeon.

But Jane lived every day knowing that they loved Miley and Kiley more. God, even their names! Miley and Kiley Riley! And there she was, plain Jane. Jane's only outstanding attribute was her academic excellence. Luckily, she never had to work hard at it. But it was just another way that she was alienated from her sisters. They excelled at sports and struggled academically, resenting Jane for her successes. Jane could never understand their interest in being part of a team. It was unappealing to her. So were sports. Just the thought of running until you felt like you might puke made the bile rise in Jane's throat.

Jane climbed up the stairs to her bedroom. Her bedroom was in the attic. While she liked having her own room and her own space, it was just another small way that her family kept her separated from them. God, trying to sleep in an attic in Alabama in the muggy summertime? Forget about it. The rest of the house had central air conditioning. Jane's room did not. They did provide her with a small window air conditioning unit. But on the hottest nights, it just could not keep up. In her research to find her birth mother, Jane often dreamed it would be someone from somewhere cold, like Minnesota. Or Canada. But her research had led her in an unexpected direction.

Some people might find it strange that she had chosen to write to Evan Tucker and not Connie Tucker directly. But Jane had her own reasons for this. Evan was one of the most successful men in town. But he was also a good father. When they were still in school, he showed up to all the events and sports games for his sons. He raised his four sons single-handedly while his wife was dying of cancer, and of course afterwards. From a young age, Jane had secretly wished that Mr. Tucker was her real dad. And maybe part of her was hoping that would be his reply to her letter, that her initial research had been all wrong about how she thought she was related to the Tuckers.

She had also mailed it to him because she had a personal, if limited, connection to him. She had had the opportunity to observe what kind of man he was. She felt like contacting him guaranteed a response. Why would a woman who already gave her up for adoption respond to an anonymous letter about a time in her life she would surely want to forget?

Jane's hunch had been accurate. She looked at the plain, male handwriting on the envelope, and then tore it open. Inside, a short, handwritten note:

I don't know why you have contacted me. I have no information for you. Best of luck in your search.

Instead of being disappointed, Jane felt elated! A response! A polite response!

Just by the act of writing back, her note had left a mark on him. It was in his head. She didn't feel like this would be the last response she would get from him.

Jane went about the rest of her week as usual. She blended in at school. It was like her super power. There was lots of being obedient and doing exactly what was expected of her. Lots of studying. Or at least that was the pretense she showed Mr. and Mrs. Riley. Always show them what they want to see, she thought. Anything else upsets them. She had asked the Rileys at the age of ten for information about her birth mother. Mrs. Riley had flipped out. They had both assured her this was her home and she was loved very much. So from then on, Jane conducted her genealogical research on her own.

4

Saturday morning found Jane at the town library, in the Local Families & Histories room. It was separated from the rest of the library by a large window, just to the right of the circulation desk. She was looking through old, yellowed scrapbooks filled with newspaper clippings. Jane wanted to double-check the birth records for Huntington Memorial Hospital for the day she was born. Of course, she had told the librarian that she was doing research for a school project. The librarian was a casual acquaintance of her mother. Couldn't have the parents getting suspicious, after all.

Jane was verifying that while three baby girls had been born the day of her birth at that hospital, only two had later appeared as happy little birth announcements identifying the families. As she took notes, she heard Evan Tucker's voice at the front desk. Her head reflexively popped up to eavesdrop. When you were the quiet girl that no one talked to, you had to pick up your information from somewhere. She had chosen to become a very good, if sometimes obtrusive, listener.

"Do you still do, uh, party planning, Jenny?" Mr. Tucker asked the librarian. He tried to keep his voice down, but it was deep and it carried throughout the small library. Jane thought it was funny how everyone in this town had more than one job. It reminded her of the Old West, when the doctor was also the dentist and the blacksmith.

"Why, Evan, yes I do. Do you have an event coming up?" Jenny Jones did not pick up on Mr. Tucker's conspiring tone, or at the least she did not even try to copy it. She drawled out Evan's name a beat too long. He was the most eligible bachelor in town. He had never given any woman an indication that he was in the market for a new wife. But that did not deter the women in town from advertising that they were available.

"I do. Uh, there isn't a date yet, I don't think. But my oldest Randy, well, he, uh. . ." Mr. Tucker was obviously uncomfortable.

"Go on, Evan," Jenny said smiling with anticipation, pushing a lock of her straight red hair behind her ear.

Jane could not believe that Jenny the librarian was actually going to make poor Mr. Tucker say it. The news was pretty obvious.

"Randy and Violet have decided to get married." Randy and Violet had been dating for five years. Poor Violet probably had begun to think 'marriage' would remain unchecked on her bucket list. The fact that two young adults that had been dating for so long were engaged made Jenny's overreaction even more out of place.

"OH MY GOD! That is such wonderful news!" Both Mr. Tucker, standing right in front of Jenny, and Jane, in the next room, jumped at the incredible increase in volume. Mr. Tucker quickly went into "shush" mode. Ironic, since that was usually the librarian's job.

"Now, they won't announce it until tonight at the Broken Wheel. But I thought it might be nice if you could help them out after that."

"Oh, of course, Evan! I would just love to."

"And you can just bill me for your usual fee. I will take care of the cost."

"Oh, of course. Thank you so much for thinking of me! Oh, I should get started right away. . ."

Jenny was used to planning kiddie birthday parties in their small town or the weddings of wealthy families in Huntington, the closest city. Jane could see her having a field day planning an event for the royalty of Oakley.

Jane realized that if she had dinner tonight at the Broken Wheel, she might get to witness some of the town's excitement first hand.

5

The Broken Wheel was the town bar and only semi-fine dining establishment, the likes of Applebee's and Chili's, with a local flair. The first thing that stood out about the place was that the whole interior was wood. No paint or wallpaper or drywall. It was all rough wood on the walls and exposed beams on the ceiling. Mrs. Riley always fretted about the cobwebs above that floated on the air currents, only one end attached to the beams. Maybe she thought they would pick that moment to detach and land in her soup.

Coming in the door, the bar ran along the right side, along with the entrance to the kitchen and the hallway to the bathrooms. The jukebox was next to the door on the left, but it was hooked into the speaker system and played throughout the place. Wood tables and low back wooden chairs were scattered about the rest of the restaurant, except for the far left corner that was cleared for a small dance floor. If the tables had been lined up in orderly rows this morning, no one could tell that at this point in the evening.

No one under 21 was allowed in by themselves, although they could come in if they were with their family having dinner.

Especially prohibited was any underage individual known as a troublemaker in town. So, naturally, Jane could come in and eat whenever she liked at only 18, and no one ever batted an eye. She guessed there were two reasons for this. One was that she was Jane Riley. Straight A's. Honor Roll Student. Expected to graduate at the top of her class. Clean record.

Except for that one detention she got for running in the classroom in fourth grade during indoor recess. But that had not even been Jane's fault. Another girl had taken her favorite stuffed animal and Jane was just in pursuit, trying to get it back. But the teacher wouldn't listen to reason.

The second reason she was probably allowed to break the age rule at the Broken Wheel was because Donna worked there. Donna Sizemore was a waitress at the Broken Wheel by night, and by morning she worked at the Town Diner, just as Jane did. Everyone in town referred to it as just the Diner. Jane had accumulated so many credits in high school that the last semester she was taking off mornings to work and only going to class in the afternoon. The Rileys agreed to let her work so that she could save more money for college. Jane had taken the job so that she wouldn't die from the monotonous boredom of her life.

Jane didn't really have any girlfriends her own age. Donna was the closest thing she had to a best friend. The good part about that was Donna had twice as much life experience as someone her own age would have.

Yep. The best students can totally get away with murder. Too bad they have no idea how to have fun.

Tonight, Jane sat unassumingly in the corner, munching her cheeseburger and fries. She was wearing a brown T-shirt with pink lettering. Her long brown hair hung just past her shoulders. She blended right into the wood walls. Jane sat at a table all by herself, but all the extra chairs had already been shuffled to other, full tables. The place was *packed* tonight. The whole town clearly knew that this news was coming and had already started drinking hard at the pre-celebration.

The Tuckers were already seated and enjoying their own cheeseburgers when Jane had arrived. Violet sat among them, on Randy's left. She was a tall, thin woman with blond wavy hair that she usually wore with the top pulled back so that it would not fall into her eyes. Tonight she wore a fancy purple dress for this special occasion. She looked very comfortable among the five men. She had had many years to get acclimated.

Donna had assured Jane that she hadn't missed any excitement yet. The Tuckers sat there smiling, so happy. Jane wondered how big a hole it left in the evening that the boys' mother was not there to share in the event. Violet would have it easier—no mother-in-law to deal with. But she would have Jenny the wedding planner instead, so it might be a toss-up.

Jane couldn't remember the last time her, Mr. and Mrs. Riley, and her sisters had all gone out to eat together as a family.

Oh, maybe when Miley & Kiley had been part of the State Championship Junior Cheerleading Team. Jane supposed they might all go out together after her graduation that was soon approaching.

Jane's family rarely even ate dinner together at home. Usually Mr. and Mrs. Riley were at some school event for M or K, or were working late. Even if they were all home at dinnertime, they did not sit down for a big family meal. They tended to all prepare foods for each of their own tastes and eat separately anyway.

But the Tuckers, they talked and smiled and celebrated. Everyone in the bar did. Jane was a little envious of them all. She watched the events and committed them to memory like a modern day anthropologist. But she was always on the outside looking in, even with her own family.

The announcement from Mr. Tucker and Randy and an obviously tipsy Violet made the entire celebration official. Jane's eyes followed Donna's round frame as she scooted around from behind the end of the bar carrying two pitchers of beer. Jane wondered if Donna ever bumped into the wall and got splinters. Jane would have to ask her later. Donna's wild, curly brown hair was stacked on top of her head as usual, with a pen sticking out of it. It always looked just a shade too dark to be natural, as Donna claimed she had to color it to hide the gray hairs that were leading an assault on her waning youth. On most days at the Diner, she would lose her pen in her hair. Sometimes two of them.

Donna took the beer over to the Tuckers' table and congratulated the happy couple. Jane watched the party for a few more minutes. Then, getting up to leave, she grabbed her keys off the table. The place was getting fuller by the minute. Obviously those who were here for the announcement had called all their friends to come down and join in the party. The music was getting louder, too. Jane was beginning to get concerned that there could be a bar fight brewing.

Halfway to the door, like a sexy angel sent down from heaven, Wade Tucker blocked her path.

"You can't be leaving so soon. The party is just getting started. And with all the effort it took to sneak in here by yourself—" His warm breath smelled like beer as it hit her face.

"I don't have to sneak in anywhere." The party atmosphere made her bold.

"That is a shame, Janie Riley. I was beginning to think you were a real bad ass."

"I wish," she yelled back at him over the din of the crowd, even though they were right next to each other. She rocked up on the balls of her feet as she spoke so that he could hear her better. For a moment, her 5'6" frame inched closer to closing the six inch gap between them.

What was with this guy? He had never talked to her before in her life. Here he was talking to her for the second time in a week. Jane was just as miffed as she was flattered. Maybe Wade showing interest in her at the town meeting wasn't a fluke after all. Jane had been telling herself the exchange had meant nothing to Wade. She hated to think that he had been thinking about her as much as she had about him. That would make him as pathetic as she was.

"Then stay, and your wish shall be granted." Wade smiled at her and she found herself smiling back. For a second, she was tempted. But remembering how lonesome she had been all by herself in the corner, her determination was again steadfast.

"I'm here all by myself. I should be going... Congratulations to your family." She started to push past him. He wrapped his huge, rough hand gently around her tiny, soft bicep, just below the sleeve of her shirt.

"I'm here. You can hang out with me." Jane had not expected that. Suddenly she had tunnel hearing. Wade was the only one she could hear. They all lived here in the South, but somehow Wade's voice had a beautiful slow lilt, a twang more magnificent than all the others. Maybe it was how he attracted all the women. It was sure working on her.

But Jane tried to fight to bring reason back into their conversation.

"You have the whole town to hang out with," Jane replied, shaking her head. She felt as though she had to convince him not to want to hang out with her. Didn't he realize it would cost him in cool points?

"But I want to hang out with you."

"You are only saying that because you are drunk."

"If you had ever seen me drunk, you would know that I am not now."

They locked eyes. They looked at each other and said nothing.

"So if I stay, then what?" Jane managed to shrug her shoulders, even with Wade gripping her arm.

"We dance." He watched her face for a reaction.

"But I can't dance," Jane replied in a monotone, even though her heart had begun to race.

"I can," Wade's mouth contorted into an impish grin and his eyebrows jumped above his eyes.

In spite of herself, she let Wade lead her further into the bar. She jammed the thick wad of keys into the front pocket of her jeans, so they wouldn't get lost. The deadbolt key for her house jammed uncomfortably into her thigh.

"Step one. Drink this."

Jane hadn't seen where Wade had grabbed the bottle of beer from that he was shoving in her face.

"I don't drink."

"You could."

Jane made the mistake of smelling the beer as she poured a large swallow into her mouth. It smelled yeasty, but instead of sweet like bread, it was bitter. Mistake number two: she let it stay in her mouth long enough to taste it. She forced it down and then gagged a little.

"Beer tastes horrible!" she screamed to Wade. He was laughing at her.

"The first sip always tastes bad. It tastes better the more you have."

Jane eyed him skeptically and took another swig.

"You liar. That tasted even worse!"

"But I made you drink more!" Wade said, and then he winked at her.

Jane took a few more sips. Wade set the mostly full bottle down and led her over to the closest thing the bar had to a dance floor.

Wade started to move in front of her, and Jane just stood there looking like a dork in front of him. Part of her was scared. The other part was fascinated by how he could actually move in jeans that tight. They accentuated all his good assets, front and back. She was always attracted to a man with a nice round butt.

"You aren't even trying! Here."

With that, Wade pulled Jane close to him. Now her out-of-style baggy jeans were touching his tight, sexy ones. His hot beer breath and her hot beer breath mingled together in a strange rhythm. Every place that Jane's body touched Wade's there was muscle. She kept her hands on Wade's shoulders, but his hands were all over her body. And God help her, it felt good.

"Do you have a knife in your pocket, or are you just happy to see me?" Wade asked her.

"My keys."

In response, Wade spun her around and started dancing behind her. He rubbed up against her ass in a very delicious way. Jane was torn whether to be self-conscious or to use her assets to their best abilities. Self-consciousness lost out. She actually, in this moment in time, felt like a real teenager having a real teenager experience. It was like in the past she had been a wooden Pinocchio of a teenager. Tonight she was becoming a real girl.

Another song started on the jukebox. Jane looked around to see who was watching them. But no one seemed to be. They were all so involved in their own conversations and drinking, they weren't even looking at Jane or Wade. Was Jane the only one who watched everyone around her so closely? The sad reality dawning on her might be yes.

It was hot on the dance floor with so many bodies so close together.

Wade's lips touched her neck, already damp and no doubt salty with sweat. He kissed her neck and his lips moved up to her ear.

"Do you feel like a bad ass yet?" he spoke in her ear.

"I feel like *you* are a bad ass," Jane replied. As she said it, something inside of her seemed to catch on fire. She never wanted this moment to end.

"Same thing, Janie Riley."

She wanted to ask him why he always referred to her that way, with both first and last name, and with a familiar nickname that no one actually used. But she had to try to remember that she had feet as Wade spun her around to face him. Could someone be drunk off six swallows of beer? Or was this just the intoxicating effect of Wade, oh so close. Jane didn't know.

Being this close, she couldn't help but study his face. The tiny bags that were usually under each of his hooded eyes seemed to get bigger when he drank.

"Hey, Hot Shot." Donna was suddenly right next to Wade, carrying her tray. "No more alcohol for the lady, capeesh?"

"Sure thing, ma'am." Wade answered her without moving an inch further from Jane's body.

Am I in trouble?, Jane thought to herself in a moment of panic. For a second her heartbeat doubled, which, how could that even be possible because it was already about to jump out of her chest. Is this what a heart attack feels like?

Sensing her tension, Wade put his hands on the sides of her head and leaned down to close the distance between their heights. He placed his lips on hers. And Jane not only forgot about Donna, she also forgot her own name. Wade parted his lips and seemed encouraged when Jane did the same. Little did he know she was only copying his every move, hoping it wouldn't give her inexperience away. As his tongue slipped into her mouth her whole body began to sing and go on a sort of autopilot. His tongue explored her mouth. This night was suddenly getting real very fast. An actual part of him was inside of her. This made Jane instantly think about other parts of him that she would be alternately super happy and scared to death to have inside her.

Wade pulled away.

"Wanna get out of here? I know someplace that's a lot cooler."

Jane watched a bead of sweat run down Wade's forehead, and realized the whole bar had become one big humid sauna. Not that Jane had ever been in a sauna. But she had seen them on TV. Her own shirt was almost wet enough to be entered into a contest.

She nodded. Wade grabbed her hand and slowly started leading her through the crowd to the side door.

6

EVAN

It was such a happy night. Evan Tucker was celebrating the engagement of his oldest son to a wonderful girl. His whole family was here to toast the beginning of the next chapter of their lives together. It would feel strange to have another woman to call family again. It had been ten years that his wife had been gone. He could just imagine how Megan's eyes would have twinkled tonight. She would have had her hair up, with a few strands escaping, as they always did. A drinker only on special occasions such as this, her nose would no doubt have turned red by this time of the evening as well.

Evan had been watching his son Wade dance with the quiet girl in town. He hoped for Wade's sake she was 18 by now. He hoped for her sake she knew how to tell a guy "no".

What was her name? She had just started at the Diner. Janie Riley, that was her name. She sure was growing into a beautiful young woman. He thought she had overheard the engagement news at the library, while she was sitting in the room with all the family records. Hadn't he passed her a few days ago coming out of the post office?

Man, every time he went to pick up his mail now, he was paranoid it would contain another letter like that weird anonymous one he had received. Giving up a baby? Adopted? Why, he didn't even know anyone who was adopted. Well, hadn't one family in town adopted a baby many years ago? His own boys had still been young. Which family had that been? The Rileys. Wait. Riley. Janie Riley. Was Jane the one who had sent him the letter?

Evan jumped up from the table and removed his cell from its holder on his belt. He headed outside to make a call. Suddenly all this mystery seemed a lot more urgent. As he made his exit from the bar, he didn't see that Wade and Jane were making their own.

The gravel of the parking lot crunched under Evan's feet. He scrolled through his contact list, the phone screen illuminating his face in the night. He selected a name, and a faint ringing began on the other end of the line.

"Hey, Connie. It's Evan," he began tentatively.

"Evan, why, you never call me," she sounded surprised, but happy.

"No, usually I don't. But today is different, I guess." How could he broach the subject without upsetting her more than it already would?

"Would this have anything to do with a certain son of your's?" she hinted.

Son, Evan thought. Actually, it has to do with a daughter. But maybe she had never known the baby's gender. Then Evan's mind rewound and he realized what she was getting at.

"Of course, ya. Randy and Violet's engagement. I guess you heard. Small towns and all."

"It was so nice of you to call and invite me to the wedding yourself. When is the big day?"

"Oh, uh, the kids haven't picked one yet."

"Then I'm guessing that is not really the reason you called, then," Connie stated in a manner that told Evan he better get to the point. He had forgotten how sharp Connie was. He was feeling more positive every second that Jane probably was her daughter. There was nothing to do but dive in and broach the subject. The worst that could happen was that he would have one less person to feed at the reception.

"Connie, I'm calling because I got a weird, anonymous letter the other day that said you had once given a baby up for adoption years ago. Is that true?"

Dead silence. Evan probably should have come up with a more gentle way to ask. But at this moment he hadn't wanted to waste the time. He wanted to know now if his son was getting friendly with another member of the family or not.

"Evan, I can't believe you would ask me that. I can't believe you would ever think that I would. . ."

"Look, I know this is a difficult subject, but there is someone out there who just wants to know where they come from. Think of how much it would mean to them..."

"You better think before you call me again, Evan Tucker." The call ended with a receiver slamming down loudly on the other end.

Evan headed back to the bar to find those kids. He tried to figure out what relation Wade and Jane might possibly be in his head. All the beers he had kicked back tonight made it more difficult. He wasn't a spring chicken anymore.

He had been wrong. The worst that could happen would not be that Connie would be mad at him. The worst that could happen was that he would poison Connie to ever wanting to reconnect with her child.

7

JANE

Wade's hand felt hot in Jane's as he guided her down the dirt path behind the bar that led into the woods. The moonless night gave no indication of where they were headed. She was alternating between fear and excitement. She felt the hard packed dirt beneath her shoes. If Wade Tucker was a serial killer, she was sure she would have heard about it by now.

Unless, of course, she hadn't because he had silenced all his victims.

"Where are we going?"

"Like I told you, to cool off."

With that, they turned a corner, emerging from the woods. A far off yard light could be seen shining on the other end of the lake before them.

"You ever been skinny dippin'?" The drop in his voice when he said the words sent a tremor down Jane's spine.

"What do you think?" she answered his question with a question. Her voice quavered with what should have been nervousness, but was closer to intense curiosity.

"C'mon, Janie Riley. Follow me," Wade chuckled as he began to undress in the almost complete darkness.

The gentle waves of the lake hitting the shore and the music drifting down from the bar were the only sounds. But Jane could not hear them over the beating of her heart.

"You know, if you are still dressed once I'm in the water, I have nothing to do but watch you get undressed. And my eyes are adjusting to the darkness as we speak."

Jane could hear the sly smile in his voice. But it did the trick. She started stripping as quickly as possible. When she heard Wade hit the water, she was only a few steps behind him. She walked along the bottom of the pond, her feet unsteady on the stones. The water near Wade was thankfully deep enough to just cover her breasts.

"Ahhh, ya. That feels much better." Wade said as he came back up in the water and ran his hands through his wet hair. Jane could make out the well-defined muscles of his chest as he came toward her. He put his hands on her arms.

"Don't you feel nice & cool now?"

"No, I think I'm actually getting warmer."

Wade let out a low chuckle as he came closer to her.

"I could see how that might happen." Wade closed in on her and kissed her again. Jane thought her heart would beat out of her chest as he wrapped his arms around her back and pushed the two of them closer together. Her burning breasts pushed against his hard chest. When they parted to breathe, Jane looked up into Wade's face.

"This all feels like I'm in a movie."

"I hope it feels more real than that. 3D even."

"4D. Totally."

Their lips came together once more. His hands now more boldly explored the curves of her body. Jane felt herself straining to be closer to him. She felt his throbbing manhood against her stomach. It was so hot she felt as though it would brand her like a cattle iron.

"You want to, right? I mean, we are here, already in our birthday suits." It was the big question.

"Um." Her second of hesitation was all Wade needed to see the truth.

"Oh God. You haven't. Oh God, I shouldn't have brought you out here—" He began to push her away.

"I want to," Jane begged quickly. This made him pause.

"Really?"

"Yes, I just, uh. . ."

"It's OK. Let's get out of here. I'll take you back to my apartment."

"You have an apartment?" Jane asked, as he led her out of the water.

"Ya, just for a few months now."

"But I thought you still lived at home with your brothers?"

"I couldn't take it anymore. All us guys living on top of each other. And you may not know it to look at them, but they are some of the worst practical jokers you have ever seen."

"I could guess that." Jane wondered if his brothers were so hard on him because he was so handsome. All the brothers were nice looking, but Wade looked like a male underwear model among them. Wade had also been some kind of baseball star back in high school. She was sure that probably helped to fuel sibling rivalries as well.

"Josh gave me a purple nurple so hard that I needed stitches to hold on my left nipple. See there!" Jane squinted in the dark, imagining how funny his fine physique would look with only one nipple.

"That was the last straw. I got my own place. Sure, I'm still at the farm for work, for meals, to do my laundry. But at night, I can have peace and quiet to myself. I can catch whatever I want on TV. I can bring girls home," he winked at Jane. "But God help me if I forget one night to lock my damn door. Those damn brothers of mine. I woke up in a bed full of shaving cream. I had to buy a whole new mattress!"

Jane couldn't help laughing as she pulled the last of her clothes on and slipped her sandy feet into her shoes.

"Why, I'm not sure I have ever heard you laugh before, Janie Riley."

"Why do you always call me that?"

"Janie Riley? Well, that's your name, isn't it?"

Choosing to dodge the obvious answer, Jane replied, "Why do you call me Janie? And always with my last name?"

"Gee, I don't know. What do you want me to call you?"

"Just plain Jane."

"Oh, but there is nothing plain about you, Jane."

She wondered what he meant by that. He smiled and placed his hand on her back as they walked up the path toward the bar. She could feel her wet hair dripping onto the shoulders of her shirt.

This thing with Wade was all developing so fast that she didn't have time to be anxious. Her life was finally happening! Normally she planned her life down to the very last detail. It was so refreshing to be spontaneous and just follow this gorgeous boy wherever he wanted to lead her. Maybe that is what sex with him would be like. Like letting go and feeling free. There was only one way to find out.

It turned out that Wade's apartment was only one block down from the bar. He had walked there earlier in the afternoon, so that is how they headed back. Cars passed them on the road, some whooping and hollering "hi" to Wade as they headed home. It would be all over town tomorrow that Jane had been seen heading with Wade to his apartment. And she didn't even care.

Somehow this had become the most exciting night of her 18 years of life.

After walking up an enclosed flight of stairs, Wade slid his key into the lock and gave it a turn. He flicked on the light switch just inside the door. A tiny apartment was suddenly illuminated before their eyes. It looked like a total bachelor pad, complete with video game systems and a mini fridge next to a leather recliner that no doubt held only beer. She had to give him credit. It was a neat space. No dirty underwear strewn about. Maybe he had cleaned it up in anticipation of bringing a girl home, she thought.

"What do you think?" he said, spreading his arms proudly.

"Neater than I expected," she said truthfully. "It actually reminds me of my attic bedroom at home."

"You live in an attic in Alabama? Rough."

"Ya, tell me about it."

"Are you thirsty? All I have is beer and water."

"I'll take a beer."

"Really?" He eyed her skeptically.

"A few sips. You can finish it for me." He handed her the beer. She did as she said. She was hoping to drown any remaining nerves that may interfere with her good time.

They both sat on the edge of the bed on the same side. They sat quietly until Wade spoke.

"I love how your hair is all wavy from the water now," he said, pushing her hair behind her ear and began to kiss her again. Jane doubted very much that her hair looked good. But she was distracted as the fire between her legs returned.

"Now, are you sure this is what you want? I'm not in a, well, in any real hurry." He bit his bottom lip a little and the hunger inside her craved to be satisfied. Maybe that was his signature move.

"Yes. Especially now that you got me all worked up again."

"Good." Another deep kiss. Wade removed his shirt, and then Jane's.

"Do you have, um, you know?"

"Oh ya, ya." More kissing.

"And you'll, you know, use one."

"Yes. You sound like a public service ad." Kissing.

"I often do."

"I look forward to that."

Jane's heart stuttered at the thought that this might be more than a one-time thing.

Soon the rest of their clothes were on the floor. The lights had been turned back out. Soft moans filled the room.

Jane knew she should be scared. Any girl in her right mind would be. But the fact that the hottest guy in town had chosen to take her home tonight made her think maybe there was something special about her after all. He could have had any woman in that bar, even the married ones, but he had led *her* down to the pond.

Her thoughts raced, while her body was ready for all systems go. Those thoughts were what filled her head, until Wade entered her, and then she could think of nothing else but the sweet rhythm their bodies made together.

8

"What time is it?" Wade squinted at Jane as she got dressed. He hadn't heard her phone alarm go off, but she had had to turn on the light to find all her clothes. Realizing she couldn't show up at the Diner for work in the same clothes the whole town had seen her in the night before, she 'borrowed' a T-shirt from Wade's dresser. It had some heavy metal band logo on it. She also happened to think it might come in handy as a souvenir in case she never made it back here again.

"Time for me to head to work at the Diner."

"But it's the butt crack of dawn."

"That is what time it opens."

Actually, it being a Sunday, the Diner didn't open till 7AM. No one was getting breakfast before work like a weekday, but some customers did like to eat before church.

"Do you have a hair brush around here anywhere?" Jane asked.

"Nope. I finger-style mine." He demonstrated by moving his fingers through his short, blond hair.

"Aren't you girls supposed to keep those in your purse?" Wade continued.

"I don't carry a purse."

"Very unconventional, aren't we?" Wade paused. "Am I going to see you again?" he asked innocently.

"What?" Jane said, surprised. "I was going to ask you the same thing. I mean, I wouldn't have. But I wanted to."

"That's good we were both wondering the same thing, I guess. Turn off the light on your way out. And for God's sake, lock the door," he instructed without ever providing an answer to his own question.

As Jane closed the door behind her, she could hear Wade mumbling about shaving cream and the high cost of a new mattress.

"Hello there, bright eyes," Donna greeted Jane as she entered the Diner. The little bell on the door seemed to chime louder than usual, announcing her arrival.

The Diner was long and narrow, and located on the west end of town on Main Street. It was part of the small downtown that Oakley had. It was made up of brick buildings that all butted up to each other, except for the empty grass lots here and there in between, where fires had robbed the town of hundred year old retail space. The Diner's white counter with the gold flex ran along the left side of the room when customers came in the door. The red padded stools were tucked neatly against it, while the kitchen lay on the other side, only visible through the pass-through window for the plates. On the right side of the room were a single line of rectangular tables, pushed up tight to the wall. At prime breakfast or lunch rush, sometimes space was limited. Usually no one minded, and was happy to wait or mingle with the other customers.

When Mrs. Riley would drag her and her sisters out shopping on Saturday mornings, Jane would be about to drop from hunger and thirst. Jane would beg her to take them to the Diner for lunch. But Mrs. Riley always would say that it looked like there were no available seats. As Jane got older, she realized Mrs. Riley sometimes gave that answer without ever actually looking into the windows. But arguing with her was a wasted effort.

Jane quickly went in the back to grab her apron. There was a large closet in the back that long ago the female employees had fashioned into a locker room, except there were no lockers. Jane was still tying it when she came back up front to help Donna set up for the day.

"I thought you should know, I covered for you with your parents last night. You remember them, right? Those people who provide you with a roof over your head and a perfectly good bed to sleep in that you apparently didn't use last night. Your mother had left me a message. I called her back and assured her that you were so tired you crashed at my house last night. Although I am pretty sure I did not lend you that heinous T-shirt that you are wearing. Could you not find anything to wear that didn't scream 'I did it with Wade Tucker last night?'"

Donna finished her tirade just as the first customers strolled in. Jane gave Donna a wide-eyed, open-mouthed glare. Jane had not even had time to process her own rite of passage moment yet, and already Donna was offering up her two cents about it.

Donna handed Jane a peace offering. Instead of an olive branch, it was a hairbrush. Jane ducked into the bathroom. Just eight hours ago her hair had been wet from the lake. Then she had turned it into sex hair, fell asleep on it, and it had dried that way. Jane allowed herself a minute to study herself in the mirror. Crazy, excited eyes stared back at her. Had she really spent the night with Wade Samuel Tucker, town stud?

Donna and Jane had become fast friends when Jane had started working at the Diner, despite their age difference, or possibly because of it. Jane was quite sensitive to criticism and judgment. But she knew that Donna was lecturing her as a friend, not as a parent would.

Jane remerged from the bathroom all business.

A few hours later, Jane was beginning to drag. The long, exciting night was taking its toll on her. Luckily, it had been a very slow morning. It seemed that the whole town had partied too hardy the night before and no one made it up for breakfast, many didn't wake up for church, and some not even for lunch.

"Um, hello. Is anybody home?" Wade's smooth voice floated into the Diner.

It was not the first time a customer had caught her daydreaming today, but it might have been the most embarrassing.

"Sorry. I had a long night," Jane replied, and flashed him a smile. She had been on the lookout all morning hoping, but trying not to get her hopes up, that he would stop by.

"Really. You should tell me about it. Was he a nice guy?"

"No. He kind of has a reputation as a town bad boy. That is part of his appeal."

"Hmmm. I don't think I approve."

"Then maybe you should come by my house after work and beat him up. My parents are gone all day to a lame family reunion." Jane was surprised at how quickly she and Wade were able to trade quips as if they were in a romantic comedy movie. But Wade was as smart as a whip, and it strained Jane's brain cells to their limits to keep up with him.

"Why aren't you with them?"

"Because it's not my family." Jane delivered the line very straight, to see how he would react. Wade cocked up one eyebrow.

"I see. We will explore that more during a future session."

"So, what do you say about coming over to my house?"

"I think you should head home by yourself and rest. I have to go do some chores on the farm. But I'll see you tomorrow, OK?"

"OK." Jane tried to sound upbeat. She wasn't very good at hiding her disappointment.

9

Jane really was tired and slept for a very long time after she got home. She had Monday morning off from the Diner. Having to sit through school all day was torture. As usual, she was glad that part of her brain could do schoolwork, while other parts could daydream about more important things. No one said anything to her, which was usual. But she did notice some kids staring at her when they thought she wasn't looking. Guys and girls. She was no longer invisible. As she suspected, her Saturday night antics had not gone unnoticed.

She was surprised but very relieved when Wade was waiting for her outside of school in his red Silverado pick-up truck. He honked when she came out the door, and everyone looked. He was so obvious and he didn't even realize it. He sat there looking like a model in a Chevy truck ad, not even in a proper parking space.

And he was here for her! Jane clumsily climbed up into the high truck. It smelled like a combination of oil, dirt, and old cheeseburgers. Luckily, the oil and dirt were most prominent.

He drove her around town a couple times while he talked about his day. Jane couldn't believe she was in his truck, sitting next to him. She would sneak sideways glances at him. She could just imagine him sitting in a barn with a piece of hay sticking out of his mouth.

At the farm, there had been someone who thought they were cheated on their order. There was a sick cow. There were more stories about his brothers. Jane especially ate them up, thinking how they sounded like one of those wonderful big families from a TV sitcom.

Jane always used TV sitcoms as the norm. She didn't realize that they, indeed, were not. The talk of his family made Jane remember that she needed to stop at the post office on the way home. Wade waited in the car and she was glad he did.

She ran in and checked her post office box.

Another letter.

She opened it right in the post office. It said:

No hard evidence, but I think you are on the right track. Good luck.

Jane was elated as she stuffed the envelope into her backpack so that Wade would not recognize his own father's handwriting on the envelope. He no doubt saw the scrawl on countless invoices and work orders every day.

A second note meant the possibility of a third in the future.

As usual, no one was home when Jane got there. Wade parked his pick-up right out front at the curb. Jane almost wished Mr. and Mrs. Riley would see and have some sort of reaction. Some sign that they cared deeply for her. Being freakishly responsible had its benefits, such as long unsupervised hours in the house. But it also meant that the parents thought you were capable of taking care of yourself. They figured they did not need to offer any assistance with your life. It was a teenage girl's paradox. Being a typical teenager, Jane didn't want them butting in. But the absence of their guidance made her feel empty and unloved.

Jane gave Wade a tour of their small and simple three bedroom house. She showed him the small living room, with the LCD TV hanging on the wall and the built-in shelves on either side which held all the family pictures and knick-knacks. The carpet was boring dark gray, because Mrs. Riley was nothing if not practical. The gray showed less dirt, she had told them. The walls on either side of the shelves were brick. The other walls were painted a dark teal color. It had a dark, den quality. Jane always thought they would all enjoy the room more if it had brighter colors and a cheerier vibe. But she had never expressed that to her family.

She led him through the kitchen that was painted yellow, back to the laundry room with all the windows that overlooked the backyard. It was originally an enclosed porch, before the washer and dryer had been installed. Mrs. Riley used to spend time sitting in a lawn chair out there reading while the family's clothes tumbled dry. That is, before M & K got so busy with school activities.

Jane took Wade through the dining room, which contained the large wooden dining room table they rarely ate at. Currently, the table was covered with her father's old newspapers, M & K's school books, and a set of pom-poms. The stairs came down directly across from it.

Jane took Wade up to the second floor, where Mr. and Mrs. Riley's tidy bedroom was. The door to the bedroom that Miley & Kiley shared was covered in One Direction stickers and had a 'KEEP OUT' sign.

Then they walked up the much narrower and steeper steps to the attic that had been converted into Jane's bedroom years ago. The ceiling sloped down on the right side of the room to just above two windows that went down to the floor. And one window had the air conditioner in it. So it was really like having only one window. Her desk, with the desktop computer the Rileys had bought for her used, sat on the same side. Her bed and dresser were on the left side of the room. At the far end was a closet. In the corners were boxes of stuff she couldn't bear to part with, such as favorite old toys and old school reports. Jane had let the dark, hardwood floor with the wide, unfinished boards become dustier than usual.

Wade didn't comment on the shrine of athletic trophies and medals of M & K on the wood buffet in the dining room. And he didn't comment about Jane's collection of academic ribbons and certificates in her attic room. It was as if he sensed what a sore subject it was for her. Jane never understood why athletics earned someone metal, but academics only lead to fabric and paper. The school was literally putting more weight on sports over smarts. Jane was the only one in the history of 21st century schooling to notice this.

"Will your parents be mad that I am up here in your room?"

"My parents don't get mad at me about anything."

"Does that make them pleasant to live with?"

"No. Not particularly." Being in her own room, talking about the Rileys, Jane could not keep the sadness out of her voice. She heard it break through and was instantly very angry with herself.

"You don't have any pictures in your room."

"No, I suppose I don't."

"That's sad."

"I know." She turned and buried her head into his chest to hide the hot tears that were on the brink of spilling over. Wade raised her chin and kissed her. Their kisses were at first gentle, then became more aggressive. Jane wanted this. She wanted to lose her loneliness and pain in Wade's arms. Her passion suddenly had a purpose. It seemed to surprise Wade, but he went along with it. It seemed a repeat performance had not been his goal today, but like any red-blooded American boy, he wasn't about to say no when the opportunity presented itself.

Later, after Wade had gone home, Jane sat up in her room. She could hear the voices of her family below. They would see her coat and shoes and keys downstairs, and know that she was home. But no one came and checked. Jane knew that some of her pain was caused by self-exile. But Mr. and Mrs. Riley were *the parents*. Wasn't it their job to keep trying to include her? Jane didn't think it was her place. It hurt her heart to keep trying and being pushed away.

Her printer hummed to life on the desk as it began to print out the form for the county clerk. Wade was a distraction. Jane had to keep working on her mission to find her birth mother. Of course, she also had work and school and preparing for college. These things were all important too, she supposed. Once she filled out these forms and mailed them in, the county clerk at the courthouse would notify her when her original birth certificate was ready. She had of course given them the P.O. Box, so the Rileys would not see it. She couldn't get access to the document before. But now she was 18. With a little proper identification, she could finally get the information she so desperately craved.

Jane went to work at the Diner every morning. Wade started coming in and having breakfast daily. He always managed to come in after his father had left. Mr. Tucker would nod hello to Jane, but she never waited on him. Every business in town treated him as a special customer, so of course Donna served him his eggs and coffee every morning. And just as she did with all her customers, she served him a healthy dose of cheerfulness and town gossip.

Jane went to school in the afternoons. Final exams were coming up soon. And graduation. If Wade wasn't on the farm, he would pick her up from school. If he was, he would stop by when he was done for the day. On Fridays, Jane would wait for him at his apartment. They would celebrate the beginning of the weekend together. Then they would go out to dinner and/or a movie.

Jane was more popular at school since she started dating Wade. But Jane still didn't really talk to anyone, so she didn't notice. It was a welcome development that the mean boys who had a locker on either side of her's quit calling her "lesbian" every time she stopped to get her books. That was a big relief.

Jane's family seemed to never be home anymore. And with her stellar academic reputation, she didn't ever have to work that hard at her schoolwork. Teachers knew she was capable of "A" work, so that is what they gave her. As the quality of her effort deteriorated, no teachers seemed to notice.

10

"Is there any reason that both the movies you picked out for tonight are romantic movies?"

"Technically, they are romantic comedies. . ."

"Jane."

"What? I thought our movie night could use a break from your sci-fi/action choices."

"Hmmm," Donna growled as she placed the pizza box on the coffee table and opened it up to expose the half mushroom/pepperoni and half green pepper/ham pizza they had just picked up. Movie night had become a tradition with them in the past few months. Jane and Donna had fun spending time together. But with Donna's double work schedule, she usually didn't have much energy to go out on her usual Thursday night off. And with their age difference, it wasn't like they were going to go out and hit the bar anyway. Jane wasn't old enough to drink, and Donna worked all week at the only bar in town. She didn't want to be there on her day off. She was there enough the rest of the week.

Plus, it worked out nicely that they got together at Donna's apartment. She often fell asleep before they made it through the second movie. Once in a while, Jane did too.

Donna's one bedroom apartment was cozy. The living room had cheap brown wood paneling. It was the kind they sell in sheets at the home improvement store when you want to cover a wall quickly and easily, but not necessarily attractively. There was no barrier between the kitchen and the rest of the space. Donna had a small kitchen table, but Jane only saw her sit at it when she paid bills. Donna was always so tired when she came home that she ate on the couch in front of the television, with her feet up on the coffee table.

"You sure this choice of genre had nothing to do with all the time that you and Wade have been spending together lately?" Donna continued.

"Well, maybe," Jane made the mistake of looking Donna in the eye, which made Jane break out in a smile and blush at the thought of Wade.

"You know that I couldn't be happier that you have a boy, well man, well, your first crush in your life. I just want you to keep your head."

"Don't worry. You know there is no one more responsible than me," Jane replied.

"Oh, I know that. I also know that you are wicked smart. I can see right through you, Jane."

"Did I forget to wear my lead underwear again today? It must be at the dry cleaners," Jane deadpanned. She ran her hands over her clothes, as if checking for something.

"I see you putting on a good front. You are going to school, going to work, sleeping in your own bed at night. But on the inside, you are all ooey-gooey like caramel with hormones. When you are off alone with that boy, I have a feeling your brain totally shuts down."

"I thought he was a man."

"You are not helping your case, honey," Donna shot back.

"It's fine. Despite his reputation, Wade is a good guy. I really, *really* like him."

"This would be one of those great opportunities for your parents to step in and watch over you, as is implied by law." Donna let out an annoyed sigh.

"I'm 18 now. They don't need to."

"Just because a new month rolls over on the calendar, does not mean that their help isn't needed anymore. Not like they were so helpful before. I seriously do not know what is wrong with those people. Ignoring their own daughter."

"They have three daughters. That is just one too many, I guess," Jane said.

"I don't want to hear anymore 'poor me' out of you. And don't you doubt that if I see you make one move toward something hasty with Wade, I will not hesitate to bust him up myself."

"Donna!"

"Now, you know I speak from experience," Donna said.

"Just because you married young and it didn't work out, doesn't mean that will happen to everyone."

"But I don't even want your head *considering* that! You have already been accepted to Clark College. I don't want that boy holding you back."

"But, what good is it to head off to college and leave him behind? You know I have the grades, but I really don't care whether I make it to college or not. I don't even know what I would study," Jane replied.

"Well, I care! And lots of kids don't know. And it really doesn't matter in the real world, as long as you can slap any old degree on a job application," Donna paused. "You don't want to be 36 years old and still working at the Diner, do you?"

"I don't see anything wrong with that. It works for you."

"And I also work at the Broken Wheel, just to pay my rent, bills, and put pennies away to retire on someday."

"And you also spend all day long chatting with all your friends, which includes the whole town," Jane smiled at her, knowing Donna was a social butterfly and loved her jobs.

"Yes, but don't you think I would enjoy it a lot more if I was on the *other* side of the menu?"

Jane fell silent. She had never thought of it like that. She had just always been impressed with how open and friendly Donna was. Jane couldn't aspire to that on her best day.

"Just don't lose your head over this boy, alright?"

"Alright," Jane begrudgingly agreed, not sure if she could actually keep that promise.

"You already lost other things to him." Donna smirked.

"Ah! Personal!" Jane yelled, flinging a throw pillow at her. Donna threw her right arm out so that the pillow wouldn't hit the pizza in her left hand, but with no way to block, the pillow bounced right off her face.

Donna started the movie, and they settled in. They got up every now and then to get more pop or candy for dessert.

Jane's mind wandered as the movie made her miss Wade.

Donna had a point. But, for the first time in her life, Jane didn't feel like she was living her life all by herself, as an army of one. She felt like Wade was fighting by her side. And it didn't even feel like such a fight with him there. She knew that Wade loved her. Jane was also sure that Wade did not need to have her in his life, as she did him. She couldn't let him know how necessary his existence was to the stability of her mind and her heart.

11

WADE

"Rushing off again, I see. Any reason in particular?" a familiar voice came from behind him.

Wade was just throwing his tools into the toolbox in the bed of his truck. He was running behind. He knew Jane was sitting at his apartment waiting for him. Wade didn't used to mind the twelve hour days working on the farm. But now that Jane was in the picture, that had all changed. When he woke up in the mornings, he couldn't wait to get to the Diner to lay eyes on her innocent face.

This was a big change. He was a guy that used to sleep as late as possible. He would just smear some peanut butter on a slice of bread and fold it over, shoving it in his mouth on his way out the front door. He was always running late.

When Wade would leave Jane at the Diner, he actually would feel a little sick to his stomach when he got back in his truck to head to the farm. He chalked it up to the greasy eggs. But if Wade was honest with himself, it was more likely that he was having a visceral reaction to having to wait so long before seeing Jane again.

By the end of the day, it was pretty bad. Wade was jonesing to be with her again. Of course he wanted to have sex with her, but it was more. He also missed holding her, talking with her, watching her face light up as she talked about a favorite TV show.

Today being Friday, it was especially bad. And here Josh was trying to hold him up.

"You know. Just off to get some pussy," Wade replied, nonchalantly.

"Whatever happened to our quality time together? We used to play video games and eat burgers. And then you just abandon me for some girl," Josh whined. He was doing this on purpose. Josh could tell Wade was itching for this conversation to be over. He wanted to leave.

"You can do both those things by yourself," Wade deadpanned.

"I don't believe you are leaving to get pussy," Josh said.

"Oh, I guarantee you I will get some pussy. But, ya know, getting off is something else you can do alone." Wade was closer to Josh than any of his other brothers. They were so close in age. But they were too much alike. It resulted in a lot of butting heads. Like, say, right now.

"I don't think you are going for pussy. I think you really like this little school girl. I think you are going for more than just a quick lay."

"You're crazy. Either way, I am not hanging around talking to you anymore when I could be getting my dick wet," Wade grumbled.

"She is growing on you. You have never gone out with the same girl for more than a week. And you are so obedient. Running off to pick her up like a damn chauffer. . . I'm worried about you, man."

"Why would you be worried about me? She can't take me in a fight." Wade laughed at the image of her trying.

"No. But she could take your money. And your heart." Josh put his hand on Wade's arm to get his attention as Wade opened the door to the truck. It worked. Josh got his attention. Wade pulled Josh's hand off his arm and met his brother's eyes.

"It's not like that, man. *She* isn't like that," Wade growled. Josh had been jealous many times before of all the girls that Wade got, but he had never gone this far to interfere.

"Maybe, maybe not. Wade, you think every girl is interested in your body. But most are interested in your money, too. This whole town is poor as dirt. Everybody knows who holds the keys to the bank. She is graduating soon, right? Maybe you are her plan for economic stability," Josh finished.

Josh wasn't wearing his usual smart-ass smirk on his face. There was an earnestness in his voice that usually wasn't there. A real note of concern, but Wade didn't care.

"Never. She is the sweetest girl," Wade said, shaking his head.

"Could go sour."

"Fuck off, Bro. She isn't like that."

Wade climbed into the cab now. He slammed the door, started the truck, and gunned the accelerator. Josh disappeared in a cloud of dust and gravel behind him.

12

JANE

As Jane didn't have a car, she made Wade drive her up to Huntington, the closest city with actual big-name retail chain stores to shop for a dress to wear for graduation. Jane hated dresses. She was a jeans and T-shirt kind of girl. That is why she had to buy a dress—because she didn't own one.

Jane was wearing her snuggest jeans and T-shirt, for Wade's benefit. Jane brushed all her hair out. She brushed it from underneath, gathering the hair she needed to bind. Then she brushed the top, so that it would look smooth on top of her head. Lastly, she picked out a colored twister. Sometimes it would match her outfit; usually not. Then she expertly twisted it up into a single ponytail. She had been doing this for so many years, it was just second nature to her. She could do it in her sleep. On most mornings before school or the Diner, she had. The humidity today would give it a nice curl.

She bounced down the stairs quickly when she heard the familiar sound of his pick-up pull up outside. She threw a few things in her messenger bag, and ran out the front door. As she hopped into his truck, his eyes roamed her outfit, seemingly in approval.

Wade could afford to get a new car, something sporty. But it just wasn't practical. He did hard work during long days on the farm. He frequently had to put greasy parts in the truck bed, sometimes hook up a trailer to the hitch. It would just be plain impractical to have a car. And why get a new truck, when it would easily be scratched or dented the next day. Wade had intimated that Josh would make sure of that.

"You know this is a long drive. You aren't going to talk my ear off the whole time, are you?" Wade joked.

"It is only two hours."

"Usually my dad comes up here to run errands. I have better things to do than sit in my truck for this long."

"Huntington will be fun. Think of all the stores and restaurants they have up there! We get subjected to the commercials all the time on TV. Now we can see if they live up to the hype," Jane said.

"Hype? That's stupid. They just want your money. And it's not Huntington I need to be sold on. It's the long drive."

"Never fear. I have just the thing," she said, digging in her khaki messenger bag with a website logo on the flap.

"Oh no, why am I suddenly scared. . ."

"Ta-da!" Jane yelled, producing two recently burned CDs with homemade paper sleeves. "Road music!" She could have brought her MP3 player, but there was no way to hook into the radio in Wade's old truck.

"What? This is my truck. I'm driving. Like I am going to let *you* pick the music?"

"C'mon, please?" Jane stuck out her bottom lip at him, blinking profusely.

"What kind of bands you got on there?" Wade grabbed one from her. The truck wandered toward the shoulder, then back to the center line as he tried to study the faint blue printout.

"Just let me put it into the CD player before you get us in an accident." Jane tried to take it back, but Wade pulled it away from her.

"I don't see any metal on here. No Metallica, no Megadeth..."

"That is because they are not on there. I want to expand your musical horizons."

"Seriously? You are already trying to change me? Just like a woman." He handed her back the CD. They kissed. The truck swerved a little toward the shoulder.

"There is My Chem on here, and 30 Secs, and OLP, and..."

"Are you making this up right now?"

"No," Jane laughed back.

"Seriously?" Wade looked at her accusingly with his bedroom blue eyes.

"It is alternative. And some of it really rocks. You might like the guitars, the drums. . ."

"I'll tell you what. *One CD*. And only on the trip there. I get the radio on the way home."

"Agreed." Jane smiled at him, knowing she had won.

Jane repeatedly apologized to Wade for having to sit around and wait while she went in and out of dressing rooms. This happened at numerous stores.

For someone who never bought clothes, it was not a quick process. She had no idea what size she was, or how the dresses were supposed to look on her. All the dresses either looked like something a grandmother would wear to church or a prom dress. Thankfully, Jane had already missed prom. It was very low on her life experiences priority list. Getting a boyfriend and having sex were at the top of the list, along with knowing once and for all who her birth mother was.

"Hey, how about you try on this one on?" Wade took a particularly sexy bright red dress off the rack. He held it up in front of him and did what he must have thought was a sexy little shimmy behind it. The dance, and the fact that he thought Jane should try it on, made her laugh.

"I don't think so," she said, shaking her head.

"Why not?"

"For starters, this is the most expensive store we have been in today. And for, well, seconds, I don't think that is appropriate attire to wear to any high school graduation."

"A-tire? If you want a tire, then why are we at the mall? Let's head over to Firestone. I bet I could get you a really great deal."

"Oh, you think you are sooo funny!" Jane smirked at him.

"And I think you should try on this dress."

"Fine!" Jane grabbed the dress and huffed off in the direction of the dressing rooms.

"How is it going?" Wade yelled through the door after five minutes.

"This is the wrong size. It is way too tight."

"Let me be the judge of that."

"OK," Jane replied tentatively, as she opened the door to the dressing room. She brushed her hands along the sides of the dress, still complaining. By the time she looked up to see why Wade had not said anything in response, he had just picked his chin back up off the floor.

"Oh, Honey. That is the perfect size."

"But, I can barely move in it. And it emphasizes my lack of boobs."

"Oh, I would say everything looks just fine in that dress."

"But I can't wear it to graduation."

"Oh, believe me. You can wear that dress anywhere you want to. Imagine walking into the Broken Wheel. All eyes would be on you." Wade stood there rubbing his slightly stubbly chin as he studied her.

"Imagine the tips I could get at the Diner." Jane fidgeted in the dress.

"You should get it. You could wear it to Randy and Violet's wedding."

Did this mean he wanted her as his date for the wedding?

"I can't afford it."

"Then I will buy it for you." He could no longer resist keeping his hands off her. They traced the shape of her waist down to her hips, just above where the hem ended mid-thigh.

"I can't let you do that."

"Oh, I insist." And he kissed her so passionately that Jane got lightheaded and a little unsteady when he released her so she could go back to change.

"You really don't think people will laugh at me in this dress?" Jane asked as she carried the bag out of the store minutes later.

"No, that is not the reaction you will get. Guaranteed." Wade smiled and kissed her again.

Jane finally picked out a simple but not grandma-style black dress for graduation. She mostly chose that dress because after six hours of power shopping, her and Wade were both famished. After a nice dinner at a restaurant that had a wider variety of menu items than the two establishments in Oakley, they headed back.

They listened to Wade's music on the way home, but he did admit that he kind of liked some of Jane's music. He dropped her off at home just before midnight.

"Isn't that every guy's nightmare? To have to sit around while his girlfriend shops for clothes?"

"To tell you the truth, I was enjoying seeing your beautiful body in all those fine clothes."

"Oh" was all Jane replied as she kissed him goodnight and climbed out of his truck.

Jane waved at him as he pulled away, the catalytic converter giving its usual vibration. She listened to the sound of his truck disappear into the distance. She hung outside for a minute, enjoying nature. The nights were still cool. The grass under her sneakers was still green and soft. In another month, it would be parched and brown. The sky was clear. Jane looked up at all the stars. As a kid, she had attended a community education class on astronomy and learned all the constellations. It was a shame that she had already forgotten them all.

Jane really, really liked Wade. Being truthful to herself, the word 'love' always popped into her brain. But she was very careful not to say it out loud; not to Donna, and especially not to Wade. She only wished that she knew how he felt about her.

They were together all the time. The whole town saw them going out. He wasn't trying to hide her away in his apartment. Tonight he had bought her a dress to wear to his brother's wedding, months away. Didn't that show that she was important to him? Were they 'going steady'? They had never talked about it. And did people even use that term anymore? Maybe she was too much like a 1950's school girl waiting to be pinned by her boyfriend. That sounded like something she had seen on Happy Days once.

Jane made her way to the front door. She took her wad of keys out of her pocket with her right hand, the cluster of plastic shopping bags filled with dresses, shoes, and accessories crinkling in her left. She could see a light on through the living room window. M & K seemed to still be up watching television.

As Jane came in the door, the girls surprised her by wanting to see what she had bought. After they saw the red dress, she knew she would have to hide it well in her room to prevent unauthorized sister theft.

13

The letter came on a Thursday that the records were ready for Jane at the Huntington County courthouse. Friday morning she took off work and drove to Huntington. Donna let her borrow her car to make the drive.

"Now, tell me again why it is so important for you to find out this information?" Donna had asked her at her house the night before, when Jane had come to pick up the keys. Jane would have been offended if anyone else had asked her that question. But Donna could get away with it. And Jane believed that Donna seriously did want to understand why Jane had this compulsion to know. Donna sometimes tried to step in with advice and be the mother she didn't think Mrs. Riley was. As far as Jane's relationship with Mrs. Riley, Donna was probably right that someone needed to represent that role in Jane's life. When Jane didn't respond right away, Donna continued.

"You can't go back in time. You can't make her keep you and raise you. This info isn't going to instantly turn Mrs. Riley into the mother of the year. You aren't going to feel instantly better. Why don't you just leave things be as they are?" Donna pleaded, her blue eyes meeting Jane's.

"Because, things suck as they are. I hate not knowing. I'm sorry, but you were raised with two biological parents who loved you. I won't be able to make sense of the world until I understand my place in it."

"There you go, being all smart again. Throwing around those five dollar words and being all philosophical. Well, I sure do hope you find what you are looking for in that old paperwork." Donna leaned in and hugged her.

"I do too." They both knew they were not talking about just a name.

Jane put her light brown hair up in its usual ponytail this morning. She was too nervous to do anything else with it. She had been thinking so much about her day trip that she stopped in the middle of her familiar twisting motion with the hair twister, and had to redo it. Twice. She threw on her favorite jeans. Then she took them off again. If today somehow ended badly, she didn't want to have to believe that the jeans were cursed in some way. She didn't want to not be able to wear them again. They were really, really comfy. She put on an old pair of jeans and a T-shirt with no emotional attachment. The day was still cool with the absence of the sun, so she grabbed her green army jacket to wear.

Jane left her house early and while it was still dark outside, as if she was going to work, so that the Rileys would not suspect anything. As usual, they were still sound asleep when she left. She noticed Mr. Riley had fallen asleep on the couch watching television again.

She walked to Donna's house instead of the Diner and left the city limits of Oakley before the sun was up. Jane had to remember to press the brakes firmly and early. Donna had warned her that they needed to be repaired. If she didn't remember, the screeching would remind her just a little too late, making her adrenaline kick in and her heart speed up as she prayed for the car to stop in time. The prayers seemed to be working. But the two cans of Coke, package of little chocolate donuts, and adrenaline were not helping her anxiety. Jane kept asking herself, "What am I so scared of?" and, "Why *do* I need to know?" Jane seemed to settle on "Because I'm lonely" as an answer to the second question before she turned all her thoughts to how full her bladder was and the lack of gas stations on North 223.

Jane found the courthouse all right. She did get lost in the parking lot, then again once she was inside the courthouse. It was a small building, but it seemed to have had at least three main additions over the years that made it have three different sets of elevators and many hallways that dead ended at doors that read "Employees Only". Jane hoped it wouldn't be a metaphor for how her whole day would go.

Finally Jane found the right desk to obtain her paperwork. But, as was typical with government agencies, she had to wait. That particular department wouldn't be open for another half an hour. Jane supposed normal people would go out for a cup of coffee and come back. But she didn't dare leave this office in fear of getting lost. It might take her the rest of the day to find the car again.

After what seemed like an eternity, the light popped on in the backroom. Jane checked her watch: 8:03AM. She jumped up and made herself ring the little silver bell for service. A round woman with large glasses emerged. She seemed surprised to have someone come for records so early, but she did not overflow with kindness or speed. Jane handed over her driver's license, Social Security card, school ID, and the birth certificate she had in her possession, which listed the Rileys as her parents. After more waiting, the woman emerged once again, handing Jane back the documents she had brought. Finally, the woman handed over the manila envelope Jane had been waiting for. It was thinner than Jane had expected.

In her head, she always pictured herself opening this information and finding out the news in a car or in her bedroom. But she couldn't wait that long. If she got lost in the courthouse and didn't survive to make it out, she might never find out who her real mother was.

The door for the county clerk slowly drifted shut with the closer as Jane rounded the corner into another hallway. Jane leaned back against the wall. She clawed and tore the envelope open roughly. This is not how someone should open something they need to keep for posterity, she scolded herself. But she could not help it.

In the act of violently tearing open the envelope, Jane let herself slide down the wall and sit on the floor, right in the hallway. People would think she looked foolish. People would not know. People would not realize that for the first time in her life, she definitely knew who her mother was.

Connie Leigh Tucker

So, she had been right. No surprises today. And, unfortunately, no father was named. That was not surprising, either.

Jane felt a little twinge of how anti-climactic this all had turned out to be. She guessed that next she should decide when she should try to contact her birth mother. Isn't that what came next on TV shows? Oh wait. That's right. On television, the mother usually came looking for the child they had given away. Except on that old sitcom Punky Brewster. She never did find where her mother was. But Jane already had a good idea where her mother was. Living right here in Huntington. Jane had looked her up on the Internet in past research. She had not brought the address with her today. She supposed she could consult a phone book. The courthouse surely still had one of those in one of the four sectors of the building? Or she could use the rudimentary Internet on her cell to try to look it up.

But that was too much for today. Today was gone. She had her mother's name. Connie Tucker's name. Even though she still knew nothing about her, just a name was better than no name at all. Jane had to move ahead to her next life defining event.

Graduation.

14

Graduation day came and went in a flash. Jane woke up early and spent a quiet moment alone, looking at all her academic awards and pondering what would come next. Also thinking a little about what a good time she had had with Wade the night before. That train of thought got interrupted by Miley and Kiley bursting into her room, screaming and shouting excitedly. They even jumped up and down on her bed. Jane couldn't help thinking it looked like they were conducting cheerleading practice in her room. The thought made her smile. If someone could see this scene right now, they would look like a complete and happy 'normal' family.

Their excitement actually made Jane recall Christmas mornings when they were all much younger. M & K would wake her first. They would all sneak downstairs and empty their stockings, dumping out the candy and trinkets. Then they would refill them, go back upstairs, and wake up their parents, all the while pretending they had not had a present preview.

The girls did seem genuinely happy for her today. They would be stuck in high school hell for three more years. Yes, high school was even hell for the popular girls.

Jane ate the pancakes Mr. Riley had made the family for breakfast. She couldn't remember the last time he had cooked for everyone. He even put in chocolate chips, Jane's favorite. There was bacon too. Extra crispy, just how she liked it. The best part was that Mr. and Mrs. Riley bought her a refurbished laptop to take to college with her.

Wade drove separate over to the school as there was no extra room in the Rileys' car. They had not gone anywhere as a family in so long that no one realized that having five of them in the same car was now a tight fit. Wade met Jane as she made her way into the girls' locker room to wait for the ceremony to begin.

"Look at you. Little Janie Riley, all grown up. I am so proud of you." Wade almost looked like his moist eyes might spill over.

"You make it sound like you were my kindergarten teacher or something. You didn't even know me growing up."

"Well, we all grew up in this little fish bowl of a town together. Hard not to miss time passing, even with those you only see in passing."

"Wade, is there something you are not telling me?"

"Just that I love you. See you after the ceremony." On that weird note, Wade kissed her and made his way through the crowd, followed by many girls' admiring glances.

The ceremony went quickly. Jane couldn't concentrate on anything Scotty Lottabucci, the class president, said in his speech.

Jane was very glad that she was not the one up on stage speaking. Being valedictorian, school officials had wanted her to. She talked them out of it. No one was really surprised that she didn't want to speak. After all, she was little quiet plain Jane Riley. She was sweating enough sitting in her metal folding chair that squeaked every time she fidgeted. All the bodies in the gym had made it hot like an oven. Jane could not imagine how much she would be sweating if she was up on stage in front of all these people attempting to speak right now. No wonder Scotty had giant stains in the armpits of his dress shirt that were growing bigger by the minute.

When it was Jane's turn to walk across the stage, she got her diploma and also a special award for being the valedictorian. Of course, they also took the time to announce this. In her extra time on stage, Jane looked out and saw her family cheering for her. She saw Wade give a two-fingered whistle for her. She saw that Donna was hovering in the back by the door, no doubt on her way from one job and to the other. She saw Mr. & Mrs. Riley, together and smiling. She could almost see the happy tears in Helen Riley's eyes. When Jane felt her own eyes getting moist, she hurried off the stage.

They all went out to the Broken Wheel after graduation. So had everyone else. The place was packed. It was the first time Jane's family had gotten to actually have a conversation with

Wade. M & K were totally crushing on him. So was Jane, to be truthful.

Anyone watching them would think they were the perfect American family.

15

WADE

Later, Jane escaped with Wade alone in his truck. They aimlessly drove around town for a while. A full moon shone round and bright in the sky. The night was warm and humid, but the windows of his truck were rolled all the way down. The wind coming in felt cool. Wade glanced across the bench seat at Jane. More strands of hair escaped her ponytail by the minute, and whipped at her face. She had changed after the celebration dinner, into a simple T-shirt and denim shorts combo. Her T-shirt listed her graduating class year on it. Some might have thought it uncool to wear it on your graduation day, but on Jane it somehow worked.

Wade sat mostly silent next to her.

When he asked her where she wanted to go, her answer surprised him.

A few minutes later, they were parked in one of the Tuckers' fields, just outside the village limits. It was Wade's former make-out spot, before he obtained his own apartment. It was the proposed site of the SaveRX pharmacy, since voted down by the council. Jane laid with her back against Wade's chest.

"So how does it feel to have high school behind you?"

She turned to look at him, and Wade gave her his crooked smile.

"Weird. Surreal. How did it feel for you?"

"Well, I never had a fancy ceremony like that."

"You never graduated?" Jane turned to him again, her voice high and surprised.

"I got my diploma. Just not till after I finished summer school. You see, I did something dumb and got suspended. My grades in history were so low that missing a few tests meant I failed the class."

"What dumb thing did you do?"

"Oh, I might have got caught on the roof of the school setting off fireworks with another idiot."

"That doesn't sound so bad."

"Ya, but it was like the twelfth dumb thing I had done while I was in high school."

"Did the other guy get suspended too?"

"Uh, no. He was already graduated. Josh was lucky to get off without any jail time."

"Josh? Your brother Josh?"

"Ya. I followed that damn fool anywhere growing up. And he always led me right into trouble."

"But those days are behind you now," Jane stated.

"Let's hope so," Wade replied, giving her another crooked smile when she looked up at him.

"So I am just dating a hooligan then?"

"Oh, you already knew that before you ever striped down nekid in the pond with me."

Jane turned around and punched him in the arm.

"What? You know you did it. We were both there!"

She reached up and kissed him. A quick peck grew into a more passionate embrace. Her sweet lips and eager tongue never failed to bring a rise in his jeans. He ran his hand up inside the back of her thin T-shirt. He toyed with the closure for her bra, but didn't unfasten it yet. She ran her hand over his chest, pausing to play with the small patch of blond hair at its center. He pulled away and looked at her. Her face was all questions, as if fearing she had made some sort of mistake.

"I realize now I probably shouldn't have taken you for a roll in the hay our first night out. You were young and inexperienced." Jane rolled her eyes at him and put on an unhappy face, so he clarified. "And that isn't a bad thing, trust me. I just wasn't taking all that into consideration. I was on autopilot for what I always do when I see a pretty girl. I knew that you were special, different. I should have treated you that way." He wanted to bring this up with Jane for a while. Wade had been with enough chicks to know that sex was 90% in their heads.

"Inexperienced and different. Just the way every girl wants to be described by a man she is having sex with."

"And that's the thing. It wasn't just sex. Not for me, anyway, although we treated it like that. It was always more with you. And definitely never plain. . ."

"Oh. I don't really know how to respond to that."

"You don't have to."

As their kisses became more passionate, their clothes soon did come off. Wade enjoyed the feel of the breeze blowing in the truck windows on his back, cooling the layer of sweat that he worked up as he moved inside of her. When Jane got on top of him, he missed it. But he wouldn't trade her burning little body on top of him for anything. He loved her being in charge of when she brought him inside of her and when she backed off. He had to find a way to hold on to this one.

16

EVAN

It still bothered him. Those little letters from P.O. Box 40. It was very frustrating that the post office didn't give out who paid for what box. All that info was right at their fingertips, but was confidential. It bothered him so much that he found himself in his pick-up truck this Friday morning heading up to the courthouse in Huntington to see what he could find out. He knew it was a long shot. Evan was already 99.9% sure that Janie Riley had mailed those letters. But it was the .1% curiosity that was driving him mad. He was a man who was used to people giving him the information he wanted. It didn't matter to him that this time the information wasn't his; he wanted it anyway.

Originally when he saw Wade and Janie together, he had freaked out a little. He was a big enough man to admit that to himself, if no one else. He was worried about them someday wanting to get married or having three headed babies. OK, he was worried about both those things. But a quick family tree sketch told him they would be second cousins, far enough apart that those would not be issues for them. So, then he could be happy that his second youngest son had found someone he was very fond of.

Except it did bother Evan. It bothered Evan that he knew about this family connection that already existed with Janie, and Wade seemed to not know. Should he tell Wade? Should he confront Janie about it? Should he wait and see if this was all just a crush that would fade when Janie went off to college in the fall, as no doubt someone with her grades would? These were the questions that pushed Evan down the road to Huntington today. Of course, he was going to attend to some business errands while he was in the city. It was the only way to not look suspicious to his sons. And also, the only way to write off the gas mileage for tax purposes.

Evan had been surprised, like everyone else in town had been, when Wade and Janie began dating. First of all, there was the age difference. Wade was five years older than her. They also didn't spend time in the same social circles. Wade spent a lot of his time at the bar. Evan figured Janie must spend all her time at home studying to get the grades she got. He didn't see her around town much at all. And he spent all day seeing everyone in town. It was also well-known that Wade was a philanderer. He had a new woman in his pick-up truck every week. This had only gotten worse since he had gotten his own apartment. While Evan thought that Janie might be a good influence on Wade, he was worried what kind of influence his son might be on Janie.

Wade was the one son he worried about most. Wade had the biggest issue with following the rules and taking work seriously. Evan felt like he had to watch Wade and be on his back constantly to see him exhibit the kind of behavior he expected out of a good employee. Sometimes it felt like the more he pushed, the more Wade rebelled. And Wade was getting too old for such games.

Things did not go Evan's way once he made it to the courthouse. The records clerk or secretary or whatever she was started in on filling out a request form and mailing it in. Evan assured her that he was more than capable of requesting the records in person, as evidenced by the fact that he had made the drive up there. Once she finally stopped talking about forms long enough for him to explain his story, she then admonished him for wasting her time, as he could not retrieve records that were not a direct family member of his. Evan tried to play the "she is dating my son and practically family" card as a final, desperate last resort. But when the clerk quizzed him on Jane's middle name and birthdate, he so obviously was making up facts that the clerk went back through the door to her files and let it click shut behind her. All the woman had shared was that someone had inquired about the same records exactly a week ago. If Evan wanted information, he would have to go to the source. The source that had already been here—Jane, herself.

17

JANE

Jane wasn't technically nervous to go over to Wade's house for dinner with his family. She knew that the guys would all talk and joke enough that there would never be a lull in the conversation. She knew Wade would protect her from any potential pranks from his brothers, although Jane wasn't sure who would protect Wade from them.

Finally, she decided that her uneasiness came from the newness of the situation. She had never gone with a boy to meet his parents before. She wasn't really worried that Mr. Tucker wouldn't like her. She was known as a good girl around town, albeit a little loose with his son. But Wade had earned that reputation for himself years before she came into the picture.

As expected, the dinner was full of noise as all the overgrown boys talked over each other. Randy had made chicken for dinner. Randy apparently usually cooked and was the best at it. The others belly-ached to Violet for a good fifteen minutes about how they would starve to death after she married Randy and took him away. Violet herself had brought a cherry pie for dessert. If she was hoping to have leftovers to take home, she was out of luck.

As Wade, Josh, and Pete started to clear the table and do dishes, Violet prattled on to Mr. Tucker and Jane about wedding plans. While Jane liked having another female to talk with, she had not the first idea how one planned a wedding or why it was important what colors you chose. Why did the bridesmaid dresses, flowers, decorations, and invitations all have to match? Hadn't anyone in the history of the world ever had a rainbow wedding? Violet was probably one of those people who would buy Fiestaware in only one color.

Randy and Violet began to discuss in greater depth which deposits were due next week and what orders still needed to be placed for the September wedding. As they became involved in their own wedding planning world, Mr. Tucker got up from the table and motioned for Jane to follow him into another room.

The old farmhouse that Mr. Tucker's grandfather had built was standing the test of time. It was very well-decorated, which Jane had assumed was an influence of the late Mrs. Tucker, until Mr. Tucker made her think otherwise.

"I love to buy antique furniture. A lot of what you see around here I picked up at the flea market or estate sales. Sometimes I will see a piece in really rough shape that has promise. I have a whole workshop set up out back where I do some refinishing. Right now I am working on some pieces for Randy and Violet's wedding gift. Don't tell them."

"Oh. I won't. I love this stuff. I am always drawn to old wood furniture too."

"Maybe I will have to show you my workshop sometime."

"Maybe."

Mr. Tucker led her into the library. He pulled the door shut behind them.

"This room is beautiful."

"Yes, I keep it that way by keeping my sons out of here. Although, in retrospect, if they had been allowed in here, maybe they would have had better grades in school."

Jane surveyed the collection of books. She looked over at Mr. Tucker, sensing he was waiting to gain her attention.

"Jane, there is something I want to talk to you about. Something, delicate." He paused. "I know you are the one who sent me the letters."

"What letters?" Jane didn't know how he knew. She decided to play it cool until she could see where this was headed.

"I—I received anonymous letters about an adoption that may have happened in my family. Being the only adopted kid in town that I could think of, I assumed it was you."

Damn small towns.

"Did the letters bother you?" She tested the waters.

"No. Well, at first a little, yes."

"And now?"

"Now it just troubles me that I can't find out the truth because I am not either of the people directly involved. I am just the monkey in the middle."

"I'm sorry about that. I just thought maybe there was a story in your family that you would have heard. Plus, I think it was easier on me if someone knew what I was trying to find. If you could maybe help me."

"I tried to go to the courthouse to look at the records. But they seem to be under maximum security. It sounded like you had beat me to it."

"I did. And I was right. Connie *is* my mother. How do you think she would react to that?"

"Well, I'm afraid I might have tipped Connie off that someone was looking for her. I made a phone call, and well, she didn't react well. I'm so sorry if I have affected your chances of having a happy reunion with your, uh, real mother."

"No, that's alright. It is good to have a heads up. Plus, the fact that she didn't try to contact me in 18 years was kind of a clue that she didn't want me in her life."

"But you have the Rileys. They seem like a good, solid family."

"Yes. I suppose they do seem that way."

"Are you saying they aren't?"

"I'm saying. . . I don't know. Maybe every adopted kid wishes for a different life than the one they have. I don't know. I don't know anyone else who has been adopted."

"But you and Wade are happy?"

"Oh, yes. He is the one thing in my life that makes me very happy."

"Then I am very glad you found each other. Just to let you know, you are welcome in this house anytime."

"Thank you. That means a lot. Please—don't tell my parents. They don't know about my search."

"Sure, of course. You are an adult now, and that is your business. This will stay between you and me."

"Thank you."

"Hey, there you are! What is going on in here? Why is the door closed?" Wade asked, looking at both of them as he slid the wooden pocket doors open.

"Nothing, kid. Just giving her a tour," he said to Wade. Mr. Tucker thanked Jane for coming to dinner and wished them a good night. He left them alone.

Jane and Wade went back to Wade's apartment. He kept looking at her the whole way, as if something was on his mind. Wade finally decided to bring up what was bothering him.

"What were you and my dad talking about in the library?" Wade asked.

Jane hesitated, trying to think of the best way to explain.

"Was my dad telling you not to date me?" Wade continued.

"No. Why would he do that?" Jane said, surprised.

"Because he thinks I am not good enough for you."

"Did he say something to you?"

"No. But I have known the old man long enough to read his thoughts."

"But, that's silly," Jane tried to laugh it off.

"Is it? You are going off to college in the fall. You could get an education and go on to do anything. If you stay with me, you are just going to be stuck in small little Oakley for the rest of your life."

"I don't care what I do with my life, as long as I have you in it."

"Then what were you two talking about?"

Jane took a deep breath. "Let me start at the beginning."

Jane explained to Wade how she had known she was adopted from an early age. She tried to read his face, but could not tell if this was new information to him or if he already knew it, as his father had. Somehow that mattered to her, if he had known. It mattered if he had only gone out with her because she was the sad, lonely adopted girl in town. But she continued on. She told him about M & K, the rift their birth created between her and Mr.

and Mrs. Riley. And when they were old enough, a rift between the twins and her as well.

She continued with the desire to find her birth mother. How she hoped it would fill the empty hole in her heart. She tried to explain how Wade had helped to dull the ache of abandonment, first by her birth parents, then by her adoptive ones. She told him about her research and the trip to the courthouse to get the birth certificate with her birth mother's name. Jane had never opened up this much to Wade in the two months they had been going out. She had never opened up this much to anyone before, except maybe Donna.

"So, you are related to me?"

"Distantly."

"That is kind of cool. I mean, that you are still so near your birth family, or whatever it is called. They could have shipped you off to Alaska or Africa."

"Uh, I think they send all the African babies here... So, you are not mad that I didn't tell you sooner?"

"I do wish you would have felt that you could share such a big part of your life with me. But no, I'm not mad."

"It is great you could see it that way. I guess that is wisdom that comes with age." She kissed Wade. "Your dad was really cool about it, too."

"Wait, my dad? You talked to my dad about this stuff?" Wade was suddenly very angry. His skin started to burn red against his blond hair.

"Well, yes. It was his cousin. I just wondered if he had any information that could help me."

"I can't believe you went to my dad with this! He already buts into my life about everything. Why do you think I moved out? So that he couldn't be all up in my business anymore. Then I find out my father knows personal things about my girlfriend before I do!" He was pacing now. He squeezed his hands into tight red fists.

"But it wasn't like that," Jane pleaded, sensing a tipping point approaching. "I had contacted your father before we were even going out."

"Oh my God! You have been talking to my father about this *the whole time*! Is this about money?"

"What? No, no."

"Why not? That makes sense. Maybe you thought the adoption angle wouldn't pay out well enough, so you got me on the hook instead."

"No Wade, never. Plus, you asked me out."

"Technically, no one ever asked anyone out," he snarled. She had never seen him angry. It scared her.

"Maybe, just maybe, you were only pretending to be that innocent."

Why was he saying these words to her when he knew they were not true? He had always pursued her, not the other way around. If he wanted proof of her innocence, then he need look no further than the blood she left that first night on his sheets.

"Get out. Just get out."

"But Wade! I didn't know you felt this way. You have never even talked about your father."

"You never talked about your family either. There is a reason I don't talk about my dad. Because I don't want him knowing every damn thing about my life. Ever since my mom died, he thinks he needs to be both parents. And a shrink and a cop and a preacher too, while he is at it. And here he knew secrets about my girlfriend, right under my nose. The first girl—" Wade sat down on his bed, tired and out of venom. "Just go. We're done."

"Don't you see? You are so lucky!" Jane continued through her tears. "I have two sets of parents and no one gives a damn about me. You only have one and it sounds like he is trying to make up for that."

"Ya, so I guess none of us are happy with our lots. That's the moral. Lock the door on your way out."

Jane turned and ran out the door, not bothering to lock it or even shut it behind her. She ran down the worn stairs as fast as she could. His apartment had become like a second home to her.

The chipped white painted steps were as familiar to her as her own attic stairs. Now she was using them for the last time. She wished her vision of them wasn't distorted by her tears.

18

Wade had broken up with Jane. And while he was not mad that she might be related to him, he was mad that she was corresponding with his father behind his back. But how could she have ever known that Wade would take an interest in her? It had always been such an unexpected development. And now, as quickly as it had begun, it was over.

Jane was all tears and snot, red blotches on her face announcing her heartbreak to the world. She didn't want to go home and chance anyone in her family seeing her. Donna had the night off, but Jane didn't want consoling and ice cream. She wanted to wallow in her misery. Although the ice cream part did sound good. Jane dried her tears as best she could. She went into the gas station and bought two pints of ice cream. Chocolate chip cookie dough and cinnamon chocolate.

The great thing about the gas station clerk was that he wasn't a friend and he didn't ask questions. Jane would have had to answer a million questions from strangers if she had gone to the supermarket in this condition. Sometimes, you just want to purchase break-up ice cream in peace. The gas station was like the confessional booth at church. And Vegas. What happens in

Vegas stays in Vegas. Your purchase history at the gas station stays at the gas station. No wonder all the guys bought their beer, rolling papers, and condoms here.

Luck was on Jane's side when she got home. M & K were the only ones home, and they were in their room. Jane quietly retreated upstairs with her ice cream and a spoon. She even grabbed a straw. There was no way she could eat all that ice cream before it melted. The straw would come in handy then.

Jane marched right up to her nightstand, where a new picture of her and Wade together from graduation six days ago sat, the two faces smiling back at her. She grabbed it and ripped it into pieces. She opened her window and threw the pieces out into the night. Light from her room escaped and glinted off the glossy finish. In the few seconds she could see them before they disappeared into the darkness, they reminded her of butterflies fluttering away. She quickly deleted all the photos of Wade she had on her phone and his number, before she had a chance to change her mind. Jane sat down on her bed and waited for the heavy sadness to break her heart for good. Little did she know, that would come the next morning.

Jane was awakened by her mother earlier than she would have liked. Jane's eyes were still red and puffy from crying. Her hair was knotted up in tangles from a restless night's sleep. Mrs. Riley had her 'concerned' look on her face, and for a moment Jane thought maybe her mother had heard about her break-up with Wade, and had come to comfort her. But Jane soon realized that that was not the case.

"Come on down for breakfast now. We are all going to have a family talk."

Could any other set of words sound more ominous when strung together? Except maybe "The meteor is on a direct path for Earth" or "Seth MacFarlane has become the head of the Fox Network."

"No, Mom. I just want to stay up here." She was desperate to stay hidden in her tower of solitude.

"Come down."

"I don't feel like breakfast." That was an understatement. Her stomach protested the two pints of sugar and fat from the night before.

"No buts."

Jane played the work card. "Do you know how rare it is for me to have two Sundays off from the Diner in a row?"

"Downstairs. Now."

It wasn't exactly "now", but Jane did manage to wash her face and throw on her robe, eventually arriving at the kitchen table.

"Hey, Miley and Kiley aren't even here yet! Why did I have to hurry down?" Jane protested.

"Your father is getting them now."

Jane buried her head in her arms on the table. She could hear the approaching protests of M & K. They were noisily seated at the table as well. A plate full of pancakes sat in the middle of the table, untouched. No one even noticed.

"No reason to beat around the bush," Mr. Riley began. "Your mother and I are getting a divorce."

Jane's head popped up at the sound of the words, but she couldn't really say she was surprised. All of their late nights at work and her father's frequent nights on the couch now made more sense. M & K let out startled gasps.

"This has been coming for some time now. Your mother and I have just fallen out of love. Sometimes these things happen to adults. When you are older you will understand," Mr. Riley said.

"Yes. This will be tough on all of us. But we will get through it—," Mrs. Riley stopped abruptly. No surprise. Mr. and Mrs. Riley always present a united front in all matters. Jane assumed she was going to finish her sentence with "together". Which would be very ironic since Mrs. Riley was speaking about a divorce. Separation. A whole way of life, ending.

"Well, which of you is going to move out?" Miley asked.

"Actually, we will *all* be moving," Mr. Riley said.

"What?!" M & K yelled together.

"We are behind on our mortgage payments. We have to be out by the end of August. You girls," he motioned to M & K, "will be going with your mother and moving in with your Aunt Jamie in Huntington. She has that big old house your mother grew up in all to herself. She assured us there is plenty of space for all of you. I have accepted a new job in Jackson."

Jane sat glaring at Mr. & Mrs. Riley as the twins began to argue about having to leave friends and not wanting to move. They complained about how much more competitive it would be to make the Huntington cheer team.

Jane slid her chair back from the table, scraping it as loudly as she could. She turned and walked up the stairs without another glance behind her. And no one acknowledged her departure. No one asked if she was OK. No one offered her a pancake.

Of course, Jane knew she would be heading off to college in the fall. That was the unspoken plan downstairs. But why was it unspoken? Was plain Jane really that forgettable? Or was she just not worth their breath?

When all the noise settled downstairs, Jane expertly made her way down from her room and out the front door before anyone noticed. She herself wasn't even sure who was still home when she left.

Jane still didn't feel like talking to anyone, but she headed over to Donna's apartment anyway. She had no other means of escape. And she didn't need to talk at all. Donna had of course already heard about the break-up with Wade and the Rileys' divorce. Donna understood how fragile Jane was without Jane having to say a word. Donna just sat and hugged her. Being in Donna's arms felt safe and warm. She was just chubby enough for her hugs to feel good and nurturing. Her strong perfume stung Jane's nostrils, but she didn't mind. It actually helped to clear some of the congestion from all the crying the night before.

How had it all come to this? Just a week ago, Jane had what looked from the outside like a perfect life. A perfect boyfriend. A family who suddenly seemed to be getting it all together. Her whole future spread out ahead of her. But it had all been an illusion.

Jane's happy coming-of-age sitcom was now doing the 'very special episode'. Or worse, maybe it had been cancelled altogether.

19

Jane had thought (hoped, prayed) that when Wade heard about the Rileys' divorce, as he surely would, that he would come and get back together with her. If nothing else, that he would at least call to check on her, see if she was alright. Because she was not.

But that was not his problem anymore.

That call never came.

Part of what made being with Wade so great, was the fact that Jane felt *whole*. It wasn't just that she was happy for a change, but that he was the other part of her whole and he made her feel complete. A day just somehow doesn't seem complete until you've been close enough to a guy to smell his masculine scent. Maybe that is why days and nights without him blended together as only big chunks of living; no more, no less.

Jane continued to work at the Diner, making eye contact with customers as little as possible. Wade no longer came in. She put in her two weeks notice before she left for school. Donna was very choked up when Jane's last day came. Donna was the only one Jane would miss in Oakley. Well, and of course Wade. But

Jane tried not to think about him. She tried not to think about much of anything.

Jane began to pack up all her things. Anything she wanted to keep would have to go with her to college to fit in her tiny dorm room. Stuffed animals, old school work, and treasured toys all had to be boxed. The house had to be completely empty and neither of her parents had offered to keep any boxes for her at their new residences.

Jane ran across the address she had found on the Internet for her birth mother. She ripped it into a million little pieces and threw it out her bedroom window, to watch the pieces flutter in the wind. One thing she was positive of: she could not bear to have one more person in this life abandon or reject her. Especially the one who had started the vicious cycle in the first place.

When the day came, Mr. Riley drove her the four hours and forty-five minutes up to Clark College in Burkeville. He helped her carry her boxes into her room. He gave her a kiss and a hug, and then he was gone. Jane sat in the center of the room, surrounded by the still-sealed cardboard boxes containing her entire life, starving, and cried. She didn't know where the dining hall was or where to get her food card. She could hear other students in the hallway and knew the logical thing to do would be to ask one of them. But she just could not face anyone right now.

Due to a paperwork fluke, she had a room all to herself. Although, it would probably only feed her desire for solitude.

Jane had never felt so alone in her life.

Jane felt lost at college. Once Clark College had provided her class schedule to her and they had her money, it seemed like they had no more support for her. Where was the cheery recruiter who had assured her there would be advisers, career counselors, dorm monitors, and all sorts of other imaginary-sounding positions to support her with her academic endeavors? Jane had no idea what she wanted to major in. God, she wasn't going to join a sorority, that was for sure. She supposed she could join the college newspaper, but even that seemed pointless to her now.

Jane was on her own, to get herself up and get to her classes on time, to get her homework done. Despite her growing depression, these things were second nature to her. Her responsible behavior made her seem like she had it together more than her fellow classmates. They were not used to self-discipline or the freedom to party. They often showed up in their pajamas, late for class, sometimes with incomplete homework.

If Jane's suffering showed more outwardly, maybe someone would have reached out to offer her help. But her suffering was mostly silent and invisible to anyone who didn't already know what her regular personality should be. She wasn't walking past people in the halls missing an arm, leaving a river of blood behind her. To anyone she passed, it would just look like she was having a bad day. As such, if no one person took interest in her, then no one would realize that one day strung together into two days, which then became a week, a month. Depression was invisible. It made Jane invisible as well.

Jane just went a full hour without thinking about Wade. That must be a new record. Just yesterday, she made it a full 30 minutes without seeing his face in her mind. This morning, she got through 45 minutes (almost all of The Price is Right) without hearing his voice in her ears—oh, that sexy, fun voice.

No, I won't do that to myself, Jane thought. Even though it seemed harmless enough, letting her mind wander back to the days with him, it really only made things worse. There may be a day, sometime in the uncharted future, when she could look back on those memories without it being a problem. But for now, it hurt much less if Jane shut out all the thoughts of *him*, good and bad. If she didn't think about him, maybe she could forget that he exists altogether. That would make the pain hurt much less. If only Wade still loved her, then she wouldn't hurt at all.

You would think it would be easier to not think about him, being away from the places where it all happened. But somehow, the fact that she couldn't go back to those places made it all seem like it was a movie or someone else's dream. It was the same way with his face. She was afraid she would forget what he looked like. She had no picture to remind her. This made her mind seem to hold on to those memories even more fiercely.

Jane glanced at the clock and realized it was time to go to her on-campus job in the dining hall. The arrangement helped pay part of her tuition. It wasn't like working at the Diner. There she had been out in the dining room, if you could call it that, with the customers. Here, she was mostly in the kitchen. First, filling pans with food, then scraping and cleaning them. There were other students who worked in the kitchen as well. They were polite to Jane. But usually she was not part of their conversations.

"Hey, Jane, there is a party tonight," Sally said.

"General admission, $2," Jake added.

"Everyone welcome," said Andre.

"Eh, I don't think they mean me," Jane replied back, making a face as if she smelled something bad.

"Are you going to the party tonight?" Dan asked, as he walked into the kitchen. He had either not heard the conversation or caught only the tail end of it.

"Ya, Sally and I are," Jake answered him.

"Are you going to the party tonight, Jane?" Dan inquired.

"I'm not going. I think I'll stay in my room and catch up on some things." Jane knew while the posters around the campus said "Everyone Welcome" in thick, black copier ink, they did not mean her.

20

When Wade broke up with Jane, it was a lot like waking up from a really great dream. Actually, it was just like it. Is it possible to have a dream that lasts for two months, because that is what Jane believed happened. From dancing at the bar and skinny dipping in the lake to the dinner with his family, it felt exactly like a dream. She had the same hazy, dozy feeling. Jane also had that same euphoric, I'm too happy to still be alive feeling, like 'I'm special, and somebody likes me.' She also had that same feeling of belonging and being the same as everybody else—that feeling she had lived her whole life trying to find. She also had the same knowledge in her head that said, "This is real, this isn't a dream. This is real, I know it is," then she would always wake-up and wonder how she could be so stupid.

That's what Jane felt now. If it had all been a dream, that would explain a lot. Like why her relationship with Wade right now was the same as it was a year ago. What real proof did she have that any of it was real? A few notes scrawled in a diary—she could do that in her sleep and not even remember. Donna, her family witnessing it—simply people lost in her dream along with being lost in their own dreams.

"So now what? How do I go on after the greatest dream of all? I take a deep breath, pull back the covers, and open my eyes to see the cruel world as it really is," Jane told herself.

Jane went to her classes and did her homework. When she wasn't doing classwork or working or eating in the dining hall, she was in her small dorm room. After unpacking everything, it looked similar to her attic bedroom at home, the place where she had grown up for 18 years. The house her family didn't live at anymore. She wrote to Donna every week. Donna's reply letters were always a welcome delight. And she never mentioned *him*, so that was good.

In one of the letters, Donna wrote:

Hang in there, Honey. I know times seem tough right now, but you are sooo young. Any second the wind could blow a bug in a new direction, and the clouds could move away from the sun. Your life can totally turn around in an instant. Always remember that. (During GOOD times & BAD!)

Jane wanted to believe that, desperately. But she couldn't see now how her life would improve anytime soon. It was such a wonderful piece of wisdom, that Jane posted that letter on her bulletin board. She highlighted the passage in yellow marker, regular not fluorescent. She wished she had it as a framed cross-stitch sampler for her wall. Maybe she would learn cross-stitch so that she could make one. She had the time.

Jane had heard a song about feeling like "the last one left on Earth," by a band called Mismatched Sox. She became hooked on the lyrics. The music vibrated something in her soul. She downloaded the whole album onto her laptop, then her MP3 player.

Jane also fell in love with a kid's TV show. Other students were watching MTV and the like. Jane didn't have any extra money to pay for cable. She only got the channels she could pull out of the air. There were only two. She knew the kid's show was simple and kinda dumb. But the little blue cartoon puppy put a smile on her face. And not much else did these days.

These were the things she tried to fill up her life with now, so that she wouldn't notice the lack of friends or family or a boyfriend. Jane also tried very hard not to notice the page torn out of her day planner or the red dress hanging in the back of her closet, which now had no event to be worn to. She slipped, and wondered who Wade ended up taking to the wedding in her place. Someone older and prettier, for sure.

21

A month later was parents' weekend. Jane didn't know what to expect, so she kept her expectations low. On Friday, she got a phone call from Mrs. Riley, saying she hadn't realized it was this weekend and that she wouldn't be able to make it. A phone call was better than nothing. Which is what she got from Mr. Riley. But this didn't surprise her. Jane knew that it had always been Mrs. Riley who kept the school schedule of sports and activities on the refrigerator and reminded him about what he needed to remember. Maybe I should go live with Mr. Riley to help take care of him, Jane thought errantly.

Jane felt sure that after having been with Wade, she now felt even lonelier without him than she had when there had been no relationship at all. Live life to the fullest, they say. But Jane had tried, and been hurt in the pursuit. Jane learned that life goes along much better if you expect nothing out of it. This is especially reinforced if you put nothing into it. By talking to and knowing as few people as possible, she would not be hurt by them, nor would they be hurt by her. The art of living is something most people have a talent for, but Jane was beginning to think she did not. She used to think if she found a special person, someone who would love her, that would be the answer to her prayers. Less, it had proven not.

Jane thought she heard a knock on her door, but then decided it must have been someone else's door. No one ever came to her room. Although it was strange, because almost everyone else in her hallway usually kept their doors open. A habit that bothered Jane. She didn't want to see into their rooms, to see that their lives were fuller than hers. Over the rumble of voices in the hall, a louder knock came at her door this time.

She got up and moved across the room to the door. There was really only one surprise visitor she wanted to see. She scolded her mind for having that errant thought and her heart for doubling its beat. She opened up the door and gasped. No, it was definitely not Wade Tucker. But an older, dark-haired version was standing in front of her.

"Uh, is now a bad time? I don't have to stay long. I just wanted to check on how you are doing."

"Um, ya, OK," Jane managed to string together in her surprised state.

"Can I come in?" Mr. Tucker asked, as he hovered in the doorway.

"Oh, sure," Jane said, stepping out of his way and then shutting the door behind him.

"Nice place."

"Thanks. Um, what are you doing here? I'm sorry. I don't mean to be rude. It's just very unexpected. . . Did something happen to Wade?"

"Oh, no, no. I can't really explain it. I knew it was parents' weekend and with your's recently moving away, I didn't know if they would be able to make it up to see you. Donna wanted me to let you know that she wanted to come too, but couldn't get anyone to cover for her tonight at the Wheel."

"You've been talking to Donna?" Jane tried to think of anytime she had seen them talking to each other. They always seemed to have a strictly customer/server relationship.

"Oh, you know. We are just old friends. And every time I go out to eat, she seems to be there."

"It's funny how it always happens that way in Oakley," Jane said, shaking her head and mustering up an approximation of a smile for him.

"Are your parents here this weekend? I don't want to take any time away from them," Mr. Tucker said, concerned. He turned his head back and forth, as if Mr. and Mrs. Riley might be hiding in the corners of her tiny room and he had just missed them on first glance.

"Oh, no. They couldn't make it."

"When was the last time you got to see them?"

"Oh, when my dad brought me up here, in August." Jane tried to hide the sadness in her voice.

"Do you have a car? Do you get to leave campus much?" He sounded like a concerned father. Too bad he wasn't hers.

"No. I have a job in the dining hall and lots of homework, so that pretty much keeps me busy." And pining over your son, she added silently.

"Are you doing well in your classes?"

"Oh, yes. I think so, anyway. I am taking extra classes every semester so that I can graduate earlier. But that plan might not work out."

"Why not?"

"Because I will probably be out of money by next summer." Jane didn't know why she told Mr. Tucker this. She hadn't even talked to Mr. and Mrs. Riley about this yet, although she was sure that they must suspect as much. She had earned academic scholarships, but they didn't cover all the cost.

"Hmmm. That is a shame. What is your major?"

"I haven't actually decided yet. This semester all my classes are pre-requisites anyway."

"I guess lots of college freshmen are in the same spot as you, not knowing what they want to do."

A lull grew in the conversation. There was the obvious question for Jane to ask, although she really did not want to know the details.

"How was the wedding?" She tried to make her voice sound light and bright. After all, it had probably been the biggest, happiest event in Mr. Tucker's very routine life in a long time.

"Oh, it was just beautiful! All of it, especially Violet. I don't think I have seen a more beautiful bride, except my own wife, of course. Jenny did such a good job with the decorations, the reception hall, the food. Oh my God, there was a lot of good ol' fashioned, down home cooking. Jenny found the caterers two states away. But they had another wedding in the area the same weekend, so I guess she got a deal. The funniest part was the dancing! I can't dance. Neither can my boys. There we all were in tuxedos out on the dance floor. I must have looked like such a fool! The only one with any rhythm is Wade—" Mr. Tucker stopped himself there, realizing she didn't want that many details and that she definitely didn't want to hear about Wade.

"I'm sorry. It's a shame that you and Wade didn't work out." His voiced sounded thick, but Jane may have imagined it.

"Yes, I liked him a lot." What an understatement! But she couldn't very well stand here and tell Wade's father how she felt so empty without Wade's arms around her. She couldn't tell him how she missed making love to Wade in his apartment; how she sometimes imagined what it would be like to make love to him in her dorm room.

"It's probably not my place—"

"No, it's not," Jane cut him off. But he continued anyway.

"I want to remind you that you were the longest relationship Wade has ever had. You are the first girl he ever brought home to his family. I'd say that he cared for you a great deal, too."

Jane didn't know what to say. She reached up to scratch her cheek and realized she was crying. She was still staring at the tears on her hand when Mr. Tucker hugged her. Then she cried some more. They stood there together like that for several minutes.

"You have people that care about you, back in Oakley. They might not be the most obvious ones, but they exist. Don't ever forget that, OK?"

"OK," Jane squeaked, backing away from him, staring at the floor.

"You know, you are the first Tucker to go to college. Can you believe that?"

"Really. . . I never thought of myself as a Tucker."

"Well, you are now. And I think it is only fitting then that you should go into the family business."

"I don't know anything about farming. My dad is an accountant. My mom is a file clerk."

"Well, then I guess you better learn." A knowing smile spread across his face. "I will make you a deal. You major in agribusiness, and I will make sure your education is paid for."

"Why would you do that?"

"My experience is all in the past. My father taught me about seeds and fertilizer and fixing tractors. Now I have to have Randy program the GPS on the combine for me. I need some fresh knowledge brought into my business. Who better for that position than the smartest girl in Oakley?"

"You could send one of your sons to college."

"You don't think I tried? They don't see the point of going off to college when they already have a guaranteed job with me. Plus, I would have to hire a replacement worker while whichever one was away. Just say you'll do it."

"I do want to get a degree, but I don't want you to think I am trying to scam you for money or anything." The sting of Wade's previous accusation burned around her heart.

"I never said that. It's my money, and I can give it to whomever I choose."

Jane shrugged.

"Why not? Sure. But what will Wade think?"

"I don't care what he thinks. I am recruiting talent. If he can't understand that, then he shouldn't be a part of my business."

"Wow. I never knew you could be such a hard-ass."

"Now you know why Wade isn't my biggest fan."

"He doesn't realize all the times you were there for him. Someone who is used to that kind of attention doesn't always appreciate it."

"He needs to grow up and realize that his life could totally turn around in an instant."

Jane glanced at her highlighted letter from Donna on the bulletin board. "That is always a hard thing to remember."

"I guess I should be going. I have probably overstayed my welcome."

"I can't believe you drove all this way, just to give me money." Jane gave him a small smile. She did not have to force it. It came all on its own.

"Well, I also had some business on the way. I can write off part of the trip on my taxes."

"That kind of financial planning ought to make my job a lot easier in two and a half years."

"I'll be looking forward to it. . . Are you looking forward to Christmas break?"

"Not really."

"I guess you won't be coming back to Oakley for the holidays. Are you going to spend the holidays with your mom or your dad?"

"Neither, actually. My aunt is going to take my mom and sisters on a cruise for Christmas. My dad moved in with his mom. She is in bad health and he is taking care of her. He is doing a lot of working from home because he can't really leave her alone for long periods of time. I don't have a car to go there myself. . ."

"Oh, well. I'm sorry to hear that. You know, you could. . ." Jane could tell from his tone that he was used to warm and cuddly families who chatted about their day around the dinner table. He didn't know that the Rileys had never been that family.

"No. That's sweet, but I am not going to intrude on your Christmas. Or Wade's." She had to force out his name.

"Well, take care. Make sure you eat right, and get enough sleep, and study hard, and all that."

"Sure. No problem."

Mr. Tucker hugged Jane again, more awkwardly this time, and then he let himself out.

Jane sat on her bed for a long time trying to digest what had just transpired. Mr. Tucker had come to see her, check on her, because she was family now. He was going to help her achieve her goals. She actually had someone on her side. Is this what it was like to have a real family? She could finally see past this miserable loneliness that had dominated her existence for as long as she could remember. Jane had hope. The wind had blown a bug.

22

A few days after Mr. Tucker's visit, Jane was hit with a strange feeling. She didn't know what was wrong with her. It wasn't a headache or a stomach ache. Was it a new strain of flu? Why do I feel this way, Jane wondered. Then she realized what it was she was feeling: happiness. She hadn't felt like this in so long. She didn't remember it. She didn't have any worries, and even the worries she could think of didn't seem to bother her this fine wintery evening. The music from the radio seemed to flow into her and through her veins, electrifying her and making her glow all over. Jane wanted to capture this feeling in a bottle. She wanted to seal it up tight and lock it away in a cupboard, where she could save it for a dark, hazy day of sadness. Then she would be able to take out the bottle and remember what happiness was like.

Her depression returned, but she kept the black fog just above her, so she could manage to still breathe and move underneath it. She didn't mind staying at school instead of spending the holidays with Mr. or Mrs. Riley. She would spend the time getting a jump start on the reading for next semester's classes. It did bother her that she had to hear about everyone else's holiday plans in the classrooms and the dining hall. She would miss seeing M & K on Christmas morning and remembering the old days when they were all children instead of teenagers. She would miss the annual Christmas parade in Oakley very much. Last year she had even gotten to cover the event for the newspaper and take pictures. Donna had played Mrs. Claus. She was supposed to again this year. And Jane would miss it.

Jane went to the Mega Supermarket to stock up on ramen noodles, chocolate, and pop. She also bought herself a mini Christmas tree and some lights. Instead of buying ornaments, she bought construction paper and glue. She spent the quiet days in the dorm leading up to Christmas making homemade ornaments. It really was relaxing and great fun. Jane wished she would have thought of this when M & K were younger. Actually, she wished that Mrs. Riley had thought of it. It could have been a great bonding activity for all of them.

Jane made a few ornaments for Donna, including a Mr. and Mrs. Claus. She made them flat so that they could be mailed in an envelope. Jane had no idea if she would receive them by Christmas or not. When the tree was covered, Jane started making garland to hang along the ceiling. Then she made Chinese lanterns to hang off of the garland. She kept obsessively crafting like a crazy person until she had used up the entire package of construction paper. By that time, it was Christmas Eve night. Jane watched Santa travel the world on NORAD on her laptop until she fell asleep, never seeing Santa find Alabama.

23

Donna called Christmas morning. She apologized again for not coming to visit Jane. She repeated how every year she and her sister took turns holding the family Christmas at their houses and this year it was Donna's turn. While Donna had no kids of her own, she was never at a loss for family. Donna did receive the ornaments in time. She ended the call by promising to visit on New Year's Eve, when she would happily supply alcohol to a minor (to a respectable limit, that is).

Jane was sad when she hung up the phone. She knew it would be the highlight of her day. Her mother and sisters would be at sea, and probably out of cell phone range. She could maybe expect a call from her father, too. But it wasn't the same.

Jane had received a package of gifts from Mrs. Riley and her sisters a few days ago, via the UPS man. Mrs. Riley got her some clothes that were not quite her style, but they were passable. Jane was a tiny bit excited about a pair of yoga pants that looked like they could go from bed to class and be very comfy in the process. M & K had sent her copies of their favorite CDs, DVDs, and books. They could not even fathom on the phone when they talked to Jane how she could ever conceivably be bored at college, a place that held so many possibilities for boys and parties. But they remembered her complaints, and were thoughtful enough to provide her with some much-needed entertainment. Mr. Riley had sent her $100 in a Christmas card, and told her to buy herself what she needed most. Too bad what she needed most couldn't be purchased at a store.

Jane showered, and put on her new yoga pants. They were quite comfy indeed. She looked at the twinkling lights on her tree for a while, listening to Christmas music. She ate candy canes and chocolate as Christmas dinner. Then she took a sugar-induced nap.

A knock on the door woke her. She had been dreaming, and it made it hard for her to clear the dream fog and fully wake up. She tried to shake off the dream, something about Mr. Tucker and Donna and Oakley, as she crossed the room to the door. A sneak peek at the clock told her it was 5:15PM. She didn't even look before opening the door. She knew who it would be. The campus security officer was the only other person in the building. But why was he up here bothering her instead of downstairs at his post guarding the door like a puppy with a superiority complex?

"Hi. . . I bet you didn't think it would be me at your door."

Wade stood right in front of Jane, perfectly framed by the doorway.

And he was right. She had given up hope that every knock at her door would be him. She acted before thinking. By the time her brain had processed that she was hugging Wade, it said, "Aw hell" and went along with it. The last seven months had taken their toll on her. She didn't care why he was here. She didn't care if he was going to dump her another hundred times over. Jane wasn't going to let him go to give him the chance.

"Wow, my dad said you could use some company, but I had no idea. You must be really popular with all the guys in the building if this is how you greet everyone that knocks on your door," Wade joked. Jane wasn't in a joking mood.

"Is that why you are here? Because your dad told you to come?"

"No, I came to tell you 'Merry Christmas'."

"How did you get past the security guard?"

"It is amazing the lapse in security 20 bucks can buy a person."

"Why?"

"Why what?" Wade looked perplexed.

"Why come here to see me? Why now?"

"No one should be alone on Christmas. They could overdose on chocolate and get a tummy ache." He gestured to the pile of candy wrappers on the desk. He was trying to be cutesy like the old days. Too much had happened since then. Too much was still unsaid, unresolved.

"That was Christmas dinner."

"Dang, I should have eaten before I left Oakley."

"Why would you leave Oakley and home cooking to come see me?"

"Are you going to make me say it?"

"Say what?" There was a pause.

"This isn't how I pictured it. Aren't you ever going to invite me in?" It had eluded Jane that they were still standing in the hallway, with Jane holding Wade in a bear hug. The type of hug a five year old would give her grandpa. Not romantic at all. But there was no romance anymore, was there? Jane loosened her hug and let Wade enter her dorm room, leaving one arm around his back, lest he have thoughts of escape.

WADE

"Wow, nice decorations. Looks like you got bored."

"You could say that," Jane replied dryly.

Jane's warm little arm was wrapped around him, and the shampoo scent of her hair was drifting up his nose. It made it very difficult for Wade to remember what he had come here to say. It had been so long since she had been this close. And she seemed to be fighting his apology. Or had he not gotten to that part yet? Being in Jane's presence was really fucking with his mind.

"It looks like your room at home."

"Because I had to bring everything with me."

"Why?"

"Because I have no home to go back to."

"Oh, right." Silence. He had managed to make a painfully awkward situation more painful.

"Why are you here?" Jane asked again.

"Why do you think I am here?"

"If I knew, I wouldn't be asking you 'why' for the sixth time."

"This isn't easy." Wade looked uncomfortable for the first time since Jane had opened the door.

"Life isn't easy," Jane said coldly. It was the opening Wade needed.

"But it feels easier when I'm with you."

"Is that some kind of riddle?"

Uh oh, thought Wade. Jane *is* actually going to make me say it. She was so cute standing there, her clothes still rumpled from her nap. Her hair was all wavy, just as it had been that night they had gone skinny dipping. He had been brave that night. He had claimed her as his own. He could do it again now. If he had any brains at all, this would be the last time he would have to declare himself to her. He took a deep breath.

"I—I am trying to say 'I love you'. I made a mistake. I don't think that I should have ever broken up with you." He was pouring out his heart now.

131

"Did your dad tell you to say that?" Oh, burn. She wasn't making this easy on him. Wade's dad had given him the push to actually come today. But he didn't want to admit that to Jane. She could throw him out and refuse to ever see him again.

"Of course not. I'm here because I love you."

"And it took you seven months to figure that out? You couldn't have figured it out, say, the day after our fight? Or when my parents announced their divorce? Or before I left for college?"

"All valid points, I agree. I got angry. I got stupid. I'm sorry."

JANE

"So you don't think I am just out to get your fortune?"

"I never did. That was a thought Josh put in my head. A dumb one."

"And what happens the next time you get angry? I have—never stopped loving you, but losing you again would completely break me, into a million pieces." Jane began to cry now and Wade pulled her into his chest, inside his coat, against his soft shirt. He still had the same great smell—a mix of testosterone, cheap laundry soap, and fresh air. Jane wanted to rip his chest open and just crawl right inside. She wanted to believe everything Wade said, but it just seemed too easy.

"Oh, I couldn't bear to lose you again, either, Janie Riley, I have loved you for longer than you realize."

"You lie," Jane squeaked out through her tears.

"You are going to make me tell you everything today, aren't you?"

"On Christmas, it is better to give than to receive." It came out muffled from Wade's chest.

"I have loved you since I saw you get the French Award at the academic awards ceremony when you were a freshmen at Oakley High."

"You weren't there. You were already out of school."

"I was there with Pete."

"You couldn't remember that." Jane lifted her head to look into his eyes and decide if he was telling her the truth.

"I think I just did. You wore jeans and all the other girls wore dresses."

"You remembered me for being under-dressed?"

"I remembered you for being a brain who wasn't afraid to wear her blue jeans. You were down-to-earth. Real."

"I don't believe it. You never said a word to me until the council meeting."

"I was worried a smart girl like you wouldn't want to go out with a dumb guy like me." He seemed to believe what he was saying.

"You aren't dumb. I don't associate with dumb people."

"I was waiting for the prefect moment. That doesn't mean I wasn't watching you all those years."

"Creepy. Or romantic. I can't decide."

"Both. Always both," Wade met her watery eyes and smiled.

"You really liked me all this time?"

"Yes! Why is that so hard for you to believe?"

"Because all those years I was busy feeling lonely and ugly and unloved." Jane spat out the words.

"So you are saying I was a shy dumbass all these years to not talk to you sooner?"

"Exactly. If you were so in love with me, why did you date every other girl in town?"

"I guess I was killing time until you were old enough to think I was cool. Did it work?"

"You were always older than me. You were always cool."

"I never approached you because I figured you would just turn me down. After all, you are so smart. I'm just the town manwhore, barely made it through high school. Since I first saw you at that assembly, I have known you were the only one for me. If I had asked you out and you had turned me down, that probably would have been more than I could take. Instead, I sat on the sidelines, hoping someone else more deserving would take you off the market, ease my anxiety. But no one did. And anytime I would see you around town, you always had such a sad look on your face. You had that same look on your face that first night at the Broken Wheel. And I couldn't resist you anymore. Once I had you smiling on that dance floor, your body rubbing up against mine, I just lost all sense. I should have asked you out on a proper date, treated you like a lady."

They shared a passionate kiss, unleashing seven months of pent up sexual frustration. A twisted groan of ecstasy escaped from Jane as they parted.

"I'm so sorry. For everything. You will just have to take a chance on me. This whole long-term relationship thing is new to me. I'm not good at it," Wade said.

"It is new to me, too."

"We have to tell each other stuff this time. I had no idea what was going on in your head, about your family and stuff, until we fought. We can't do that again."

"Yes. That makes sense," Jane sniffed.

"And, I don't want to lose you again."

"So what do we do now?" Jane asked.

"Well, we both agree we *love* each other. I would say we have to get together and see what happens." He whispered the word "love", as if someone else was around to hear.

"But I am here and you are still in Oakley. How is that going to work?"

"Lots of miles on my truck, I guess. Maybe we could see about getting you a car, too."

"But I have years to be here yet," Jane reminded him.

"I have years to wait."

"Aren't you sick of waiting for me by now?"

"I would wait for you forever."

"Sounds good to me. Can you, um, stay for a while?" A while meaning 'the night'.

"Yes. I was thinking about getting a hotel room. Maybe you could come with me. We could find some place with a hot tub, or a pool," Wade said.

"But I don't know how to swim."

"Then we found something that *I* can teach *you*."

"And your dad is OK with you staying the night?"

"Well, I am a legal adult. And after the meal he is going to eat at Donna's house, I think he will probably be asleep by 8PM."

"*Your dad* is having Christmas with *Donna*?" Jane shrieked.

"Sure. Wait, you didn't know?"

"Know what?"

"You and Donna are as thick as thieves. I just thought she would have told you. Dad & Donna are dating."

"No way! She didn't tell me anything."

"Sounds like you need to make a trip to Oakley to see what is happening without you."

"I do miss the town. Even though I have no home to go back to there."

"Hey, you can always come to my place."

"You didn't feel that way last summer." Jane couldn't resist bringing up the hurt he had caused her, even though she knew it was childish. But she didn't want to keep it bottled up inside of her.

"Honestly, I was waiting for you to come back and talk to me. I didn't want to have to be the first one to break the silence. Especially since I was the one who screwed up."

"We both did. In the new spirit of complete openness and all, are you aware of the deal that your dad made with me?" Jane asked.

"I know he came to see you, but I don't know the specifics."

"He told me if I studied agribusiness, he would make sure my college was paid for, and he would have a job waiting for me after I graduate."

"Oh, Lord. I don't think I could concentrate on work with you around every day," Wade exclaimed.

"I could roll around in the barn every morning if that would make me more unappealing."

"Only if I am with you, Darlin'."

"You aren't mad?"

"Sounds boring to me, but if you want to, then go for it. Just make sure there is some time for me as well as those books," Wade drawled.

"Of course."

"I was thinking, if you still have that sexy red dress, maybe we could go out on a really nice date sometime, and you could wear it."

"I do. I would like that."

"I was thinking this might go along with it." Wade handed her a small gift-wrapped box.

"Oh, I don't have anything for you. . ."

"I will accept chocolates and paper ornaments."

"That I can do! Thank you." Jane bounced up and down. She opened the box to find a necklace with a single red teardrop gemstone hanging from it. It looked like a ruby.

"Oh, Wade. I love it." He helped her put it on.

"I missed you so bad at that wedding. I should have come and got you then."

"What stopped you?"

"I figured you were here at college partying with all your new smart friends. Then my dad came back with a report telling me that wasn't the case." Jane bowed her head.

"I was in a pretty bad place when he stopped by. And I haven't been to a single party."

"That is why you need me. I will teach you how to be a party animal yet."

"Then why did you ask the shy girl in the corner of the bar to dance if you wanted a party animal?"

"Because I could see the potential."

Jane gave him her full, beaming smile, before it dissolved into more kisses.

24

Wade did buy Jane a car, although the details of it all remained a little sketchy to her. The timing also seemed to be a little too convenient. Was it a coincidence that Jane got her car a week before Donna and Mr. Tucker announced they were getting married? With Donna asking her to be in the wedding, Jane was pretty sure that it was not, and that Wade had not acted alone.

This had all happened in February. Donna wanted to have a spring wedding, but Jenny Jones said she simply could not have all of the fabulous details hammered out in just a few months. Evan Tucker was seen as the King of Oakley. A wedding for royalty doesn't happen overnight. So it was to be a summer wedding instead.

On New Year's Eve, when Donna had come to visit, Jane asked her why she had never mentioned that she was dating Mr. Tucker in her letters.

"Oh Honey, I knew you were still hurting over Wade. I didn't want to mention anything that would make you think of him anymore than you already were."

"But you must have been dying to share your news with me. It was happy news. I could have dealt with it. . . somehow."

"I was busting a gut trying not to tell you. It was harder when we were talking on the phone. That is why I usually wrote letters."

Donna was going a little over the top for a woman in her mid 30's who had already been married once. But that had been for a short time when she was young and stupid, in front of a Justice of the Peace, wearing a Sears dress with her groom's vomit on it. She wanted to aim for something a little more highbrow this time. She had found her Prince Charming, and she wanted the fairy tale wedding to go along with it. Mr. Tucker had been so moved by his son's wedding in the fall that he was more than willing to let Donna have her fairy tale.

"Evan is so great about all the wedding details. 'Whatever you want', he says," Donna gushed to Jane. Jane had never seen Donna so happy. Jane was home for the weekend, helping Donna pick out bridesmaid dresses. They were only at the second store of the day, so Jane wasn't burned out yet.

"Guy translation: Leave me out of it! Financing two lavish weddings in one year? He must be rich." Jane made it a statement rather than a question on purpose.

"Oh, Evan doesn't like to talk about that kind of thing. He just told me that he hasn't had a pretty lady to spend money on in a while. He has to make up for lost time."

"How are the boys taking all this?" It was funny, but that is how Jane always thought of Wade and his brothers, as boys, even though they were all older than Jane herself.

"So far they seem tickled pink. Now you understand, I'm not trying to replace their mama, God rest her soul. They do get mad that I work too much and am not at home more to cook for them."

"Add me to the list. I am mad you don't come to school and cook me meals either."

"Honey, there is only so much a woman can do when limited to only a microwave." They both laughed. Jane came out of the dressing room she had been in.

"Ah, now look at that. That is a *great* dress." Donna helped Jane zip up the back.

"When I have my wedding, I am getting married in jeans," Jane said. Donna acted like she hadn't heard her. Donna continued.

"Aw, it is such a shame! This looks fabby on you, but my sister, the maid of honor, is a totally different body type than you. She is more round like me. Is it OK for the maid of honor to have a different dress than the other bridesmaids? Maybe I should do some research on the Internet."

"Ask Jenny."

"Great idea! That is why I keep you around."

Donna had wanted Jane to be her maid of honor. Jane thought that was not a good idea. She thought Donna should give the honor to flesh and blood family, her sister. Plus, Jane would be off at college too much to actively be part of the planning. But most of all, Jane had no freaking idea how to even begin to be maid of honor. She had never even been in a wedding before. There were already so many little things she had no idea about. You had to have shoes dyed to match your dress? The dress required alterations? Alterations required an appointment? There was a rehearsal? M & K had once both been flower girls for someone's wedding. Mrs. Riley must have handled all these details for them without Jane ever knowing.

The one good thing about the wedding was that Mrs. Riley, her sisters, and Mr. Riley had all been invited. Since getting the car, Jane had gone to visit him once. It seemed like an eternity since she had seen him last. He had a new haircut. It was much shorter, which showed off his receding hairline, but was much more contemporary. He had also gotten contact lenses. He had lost weight, but not totally updated his wardrobe yet. His clothes hung off of him. He tried to tuck too-big shirts into his baggy pants. Jane could only shudder at the thought of Mr. Riley hitting the dating scene. She had wanted to visit Mrs. Riley and her sisters soon as well, but that was more complicated. M & K wanted her to spend the whole weekend with them. As the wedding plans started piling up, it seemed to be more difficult to fit them into the schedule.

Jane couldn't help but daydream about them all in the same room again, all dressed up, chatting with Wade. It would be like the pretty, happy picture they had been at graduation again. But this time she prayed there would not be any fallout afterwards. Everyone was in their better place now.

25

When Jane had a two week break between spring and summer semesters, she drove to Huntington to spend a couple days with M & K. Jane didn't think of it as going to see Mrs. Riley. She found that while she really hadn't missed her presence in her life, as she had thought she would, she really did miss her sisters. They must miss her too, because she received a birthday card from them for her 19th birthday. And their calls begging her to come to visit were getting more frequent.

Jane parked her used blue Pontiac Sunfire at the curb and got out. She walked cautiously up the sidewalk of the big, old home. It seemed to be located in a district with lots of other historical homes. There was no address number on the house, so she wasn't sure if it was her aunt's or not. She had been here when she was small, but that must have been at least ten years ago. She knocked hesitantly. She waited. She knocked again, harder. It was lunchtime on a Saturday, so maybe they were all in the kitchen eating and could not hear the door. Or maybe they had forgotten she was coming at all.

Suddenly the door burst open and Jane was being hugged by two strange tall women, who were also screaming at her. It was really more of an attack than a hug. Once she backed up enough to peel them away, Jane realized that they were indeed Miley and Kiley, but they looked *so* different!

"What the hell happened to you guys?!" Jane yelled at them.

"We grew up!" Miley yelled.

"That's what happens when you don't see us for a year," Kiley added snarkily.

"Hey, it was only nine months. And I wasn't the one who went to the Caribbean for Christmas," Jane said.

"You look old too, ya know," Kiley said.

"Well, gee thanks, I guess," Jane said.

They dragged her into the house, where she joined them at the long, rectangular dining room table for lunch. Mrs. Riley and Jane's Aunt Jamie were also at the table. Jane had not seen her aunt in years. Mrs. Riley and her sisters were living here with someone that Jane considered practically a stranger. Aunt Jamie sat at the head and welcomed her. Mrs. Riley got up and gave her a quick hug before Jane was seated. They didn't say much, as no one could get a word in edgewise with Miley and Kiley in the room.

"I was thinking we could go to the mall this afternoon. You can drive us, of course. It is sooo cool that you have your own car, even if it is used. All the kids at school have their own cars, except us," Miley whined and glared at her mother.

"OK. But only if we can go to the bookstore too. And Hot Topic," Kiley added.

The mall? Jane could still remember when the twins were toddlers who required a nap every afternoon. Jane would have to tip-toe silently around the house while they slept. It seemed like just yesterday.

And here they sat. Sixteen years old and all grown up. They both must have grown at least six inches in the last year. They were the same height as Jane now, but they no doubt had more growing left to do.

"What is the deal with the hair?" Jane asked in the car, on the way to the mall. Her identical twin sisters could now be easily told apart by their strikingly different hair colors. They used to both have brown hair, just a shade or two darker than Jane's own light brown hair.

"Mom told me I couldn't dye my hair black," Kiley began, sitting in the passenger seat with long hair as dark as a crow.

"But you obviously did," Miley interrupted from the back seat.

"You are jumping ahead in *my* story!" Kiley said, frustrated.

"It's our story. Jane asked both of us."

"Everything is *always* about the both of us!" Kiley whined, throwing her hands up.

"Ah, I am starting to see the real story here. You guys wanted a little individuality?"

"Exactly!" they agreed in unison.

"This is why we miss you. You get this stuff. Mom doesn't," Kiley said earnestly.

"At our new school, no one could tell us apart. It was never a problem in Oakley. Our friends had grown up with us. It was obvious to them," Miley said.

"I wanted to dye my hair black—"

"Uh, not this again," Miley groaned.

"Mom told me I couldn't. But then on the cruise she goes and takes Miley to the salon to get her hair dyed blond!"

"They are just blond highlights. And it was a mother/daughter bonding day. You didn't want to go, remember? You wanted to stay behind and read your stinky old book."

"Poe is classic! And you guys talked about getting fingernails and toenails done, not hair," Kiley said.

"They are called manicures and pedicures. You would know that if you ever cut your's," Miley shot back.

"And that's why I don't want to be mistaken for you and your over-primped nails," Kiley directed to the back seat. "As soon as we got home, I dyed my hair black."

"Mom blew a gasket. She used permanent dye!"

"Of course I did! Why would I half-ass my own metamorphosis?"

"She keeps using big words all-the-time now. It is so annoying," Miley stage whispered to Jane in the front seat.

"I really did miss you guys. It seems like I left just when you started to get interesting," Jane said.

"We were always interesting," Miley said.

"I wish I had realized that sooner. I just always thought of you guys as a pair. M & K."

"Ya, we know. We read your diary," Kiley said.

As they walked the Huntington Square Mall, Jane got a better idea of who her sisters were as individuals. Miley, of the blond hair, was definitely more into boys, clothes, makeup—a real girly-girl. She was also more outgoing. Kiley, of the hair as dark as midnight, was more introspective. Whether it was real or part of her Goth act, Jane could not say. Miley insisted pop music was better, while Kiley was into alternative. All of the stories Miley told, she was always with her friends. Kiley's stories were the opposite, she was usually alone. Kiley seemed to be able to travel outside the safety of a group, where Miley did not yet have that confidence. Kiley was positive she wanted to be a writer when she grew up. Miley was insistent that she would be a singer.

"C'mon, Jane. Can you believe her as a singer? You remember what she used to sound like around the house," Kiley said.

"Uh, no. Actually I don't remember," Jane was a little ashamed.

"I realize I am not star material yet. I am not delusional. That is why Mom is letting me take voice lessons. And I am in choir now at school," said Miley.

"You know they will just compare you to that Mickey Mouse girl with the same name," Kiley said.

"That's why I am going to have a stage name. I am not sure what it will be yet. I am going to perform in the talent show for the county fair this summer. Oh Jane, you have to come!" Miley gushed.

"You let me know when it is, and I will do my best."

As they approached the food court, Kiley gave Jane a glaring look.

"Do we have to beg? Please buy us some frozen yogurt already."

"Yep, I hear sister bonding is not complete without it," Miley added.

"Alright. I guess that it cheaper than those earrings you were eyeballing," Jane said to Miley, giving her a playful push.

It was so strange to Jane that the girls were treating her like the cool one now, just because she was in college. She had always thought of them as the cool ones.

The wind could blow a bug, Jane thought.

As they turned sharply toward the yogurt place, a woman slammed right into Jane.

"God, look where you are going already! Geez." The woman glared at Jane and took off in a hurry. She had messy red hair and her face was all pinched with anger. She looked as though she wore that expression often, from the wrinkles starting to appear around her eyes. Jane looked at her objectively, and decided the woman probably wasn't really that old, she was just one of those people who looked old before their time.

"C'mon. I think some guys from school might be over there," said Kiley. Even in the few hours she had become reacquainted with her, Jane could tell this was very unKiley-like behavior. Miley's facial expression showed this to be true. It must be someone that Kiley *really* liked.

26

"I can't believe you are heading back to college tomorrow," whined Miley.

"Are you sure you can't stay another night?" asked Kiley.

"This is my third night here. I really need to get back to buy my books and get ready for classes."

"Ack. You are *still* such a brain," Miley said, rolling her eyes.

"If I stay another day, I might be unrecognizable," Jane said, looking at herself in the mirror in Miley and Kiley's room. Miley had convinced her to get "blond highlights", which was apparently teen girl code for going blond. They had spent all afternoon playing salon in their room on Jane. Kiley had layered on eyeliner on her until Jane looked like a relative of a raccoon. Her fingernails were each a different color, some with rhinestones or stripes. Kylie had wanted to add purple streaks to Jane's hair. Jane had agreed, until she remembered Donna's wedding. She had to decline, as she didn't think Donna would want Jane to have purple hair clashing with her orange bridesmaid dress.

Jane's text tone on her cell phone chimed. She knew it would be a response from Wade. She had just sent him a picture of her new and improved appearance. She picked it up and read his reply.

WADE: Very Avril Lavigne. I like. Stop by my apt & I will show u how much I like it. I mite show u x2.

"What did he say?" the twins both cried, trying to grab the phone out of Jane's hand. Jane had to be quick with her new fingernails to keep it from them.

"He said he liked it," Jane summarized.

"Oh, I knew it! Wade has dated a lot of blonds in the past," Miley said.

"How would you know?" Jane asked, shocked.

"Oh, it was always the gossip around town who the Tuckers were dating. We would even hear the moms gossiping about it at cheerleading practice and volleyball games," Miley informed her.

"Imagine when we heard that you had gone back to Wade's apartment with him," Kiley began.

"We were so jealous!" Miley added.

"The boy is fine," Kiley finished.

"The other moms were telling our mom that she should keep you away from Wade," Miley said.

"Really?" Jane was shocked.

"Ya. But she told them that you were a smart girl and she had raised you right, so she didn't see the need to worry," Kiley said.

"I think Mom didn't make you stop seeing him because she knew he was hot too."

"Miley!" Jane yelled.

"The boy is fine," Kiley repeated.

"Huh. She never said a word to me. I never knew about any of that," Jane said.

"Ya, Mom can be weird like that."

"Too bad you guys couldn't visit me at college sometime. That would be fun," Jane said.

"Ooo, college guys," Miley said.

"Maybe Wade could take us up there!" Kiley said.

"Uh, you would have to take that up with him," Jane said. Before the words were out of her mouth, both girls were on their phones, texting poor Wade.

Neither of them received a return text, but Jane did:

WADE: What is this about me being a shuttle bus 4 a Clark College tour? R U recruiting from in your family? Let me guess: majoring in agribusiness 2.

Jane giggled and typed back:

JANE: More like English & music.

WADE: U wud think twins wud b interestd in the same thing.

JANE: You wud think that, but no.

WADE: Still thinkin about that blond hair. Let me know when they take u out 4 a tattoo.

The girls pestered her for an answer. Jane told them Wade would think about it. And she was pretty sure that Kiley was already hiding a tattoo on her ankle.

"No matter what, I'll see you guys at the wedding. It is going to be the biggest event in Oakley since, well, the last Tucker wedding."

27

"Donna, are you sure you are feeling OK? You seem, well, a little keyed up," Jane asked.

They were at Donna's apartment, a few hours after the rehearsal dinner. Tomorrow was her big day. As Jane converted the couch into a bed, she couldn't help but be concerned for her friend.

"Oh, I know Jenny said she has all the caterers and rentals confirmed, but I keep thinking there must be something that I should be checking on!" Donna's voice was slightly hysterical with anxiety. "I mean, I have never done this before. I mean, not the right way. Oh, you know what I mean. . ."

"You should try to relax and get some sleep. By this time tomorrow, you will be Mrs. Evan Tucker."

"Oh God, thinking that will just make me worry more. Here, I have finally found the perfect man to settle down and spend my life with. When do I need his love and support the most? Why the night I am traditionally not supposed to see him. Doesn't that just figure," Donna vented. Jane was pretty sure all the neighbors were informed as well.

"It will be alright," Jane tried to soothe her, but didn't really know what to say. Jane had never been in this situation.

"But what about the weather tomorrow. First the weatherman says blinding heat. Then he says that will set off thunderstorms. *Severe* thunderstorms, that is the word he used!"

"It will be OK," Jane repeated. She didn't want to let on to Donna that she too was worried about the weather behaving for the big day.

"Oh, Jane. I don't know what I would do without you."

"You would have had a lot more tips at the Diner the past year. You would not have a car with the dent in the front bumper from when I borrowed it. You could have a life removed from teenage drama altogether. I know I wish I had that. You wouldn't have to waste time reading my letters and writing back to answer me..."

"Jane Riley. Stop all that nonsense talk now. You do not have a very clear picture of yourself. And if I find out that Wade is feeding your low self-esteem, I will punish him just as if he were my own son."

"What are you talking about? I know I get in the way of your life sometimes. It just feels good to be friends with you. You are so much—"

"If you say 'older' Jane, I will have to punish you too. I am friends with you Jane because you are a bright, intelligent, loving girl. I do not ever see my friends as a burden. You know I enjoyed working with you at the Diner. It made the time go faster. You are more valuable to me than some dumb car that never starts on Tuesdays. The teenage drama you bring into my life keeps me young. And I have never seen your letters as a waste of time. I consider it an honor to be acquainted with you."

Jane was glad to see that for the moment Donna had been distracted from her own worries. But Jane wasn't going to accept compliments without trying to prove that she was the inferior party here and did not deserve Donna's praise.

"Those things may all be true, but I have gotten way more out of our friendship than you have. It is unbalanced, in my favor."

"I would say it has always been pretty equal. You remind me of all the details I shouldn't forget, and I remind you of the big picture that you shouldn't overlook."

"You are getting philosophical. I think you should go to bed," Jane laughed it off.

"Jane, I could not love you more if you were my own daughter. As you already have two moms, that probably doesn't mean much to you. But being that I have no kids of my own, it means a lot to me."

The tears were in Jane's eyes before Donna had finished the sentence. She had no immediate comeback. She tugged at the sheets on the fold-out couch again. Finally she whispered, "Still unbalanced."

"Why? Why is it unbalanced?" Donna asked, tilting her head to the side, trying to look at Jane's face that was still looking down at the couch.

"Because you have always acted like a mother to me when no one else would." Jane barely pushed the words out before she started sobbing. Donna, who had reacted with anger through the whole argument, now wrapped her arms around Jane and began to cry too. They sat on the couch, still holding each other.

"You know," Jane finally squeaked out, "when Wade and I got back together, we made an agreement to be more open about our feelings and thoughts and stuff."

"And you think that you and I should have the same arrangement?" Donna confirmed.

Jane nodded.

"My God Jane, how much did you grow up in a year, off at that college of your's?"

"Mostly I sat around and was depressed."

"Oh, I could tell that from your letters. I was about to come up there and slap some sense into you. Here you are, all that brains and beauty. The chance of a lifetime to get a good education, make yourself into anything you want to be, and you were mooning over some boy. . ."

"I was lonely. I didn't have you or Wade or my sisters. I didn't even have the illusion of caring parents at home that I had had while I was here in Oakley."

"You could have made new friends there."

"But I couldn't. I was that far gone. And I didn't want new friends. I wanted the old ones back."

"But now you have found the sun again. No reason not to make new friends. . . You could at least try."

"I could."

"But you won't."

Jane looked around the apartment and a thought occurred to her.

"When are you moving in with Mr. Tucker?" Jane asked.

"Oh, probably in a few weeks. I was trying to get past the hustle and bustle of the wedding first."

"I guess this will probably be the last time I will spend the night at your place."

"Nonsense. When I move in with Evan, it will be my house too. And you can come stay with me anytime you like."

"Are you sure?"

"You can't be stayin' at Wade's apartment every time you come visit Oakley. Plus, he doesn't feed you as well as I do."

"Are you still keeping both of your jobs?"

"For now, although Evan doesn't want me to. He says his sons are finally old enough to handle things around the farm if he was out of town. He wants me to quit working so we can travel. Can you imagine? I have worked since I was 15! I wouldn't know what to do with myself if I didn't."

"Shouldn't that be something you guys agree on before you get married?"

"Oh, no, Honey. We have talked about it and have agreed to disagree. I suppose when the time comes he will travel some by himself and I will have to take a little time off. But it will all work itself out. . . If I can just get past the damn wedding."

"I think you should go call Evan right now. Tradition doesn't say you can't talk to the groom the night before the wedding." Jane hoped this was the case, anyway.

"Oh. You are a genius. That is why you have got to stay at college, Honey. I'm going to go call him right now!" Donna ran right off into the bedroom to call him.

"You're welcome!" Jane called after her.

"Thank you!" Donna replied.

Jane changed into her pajamas and laid down on the folded out bed. The frame squeaked repeatedly as she tried to get comfortable. Jane sent Wade a text:

JANE: R u partyin w/your dad?

She hit send.

"He's so relaxed, he was already asleep!" Donna yelled from the bedroom.

Jane chuckled in response as her phone chimed:

WADE: We r partyin w/o him. Luv u.

JANE: Dont party 2 hard. Love u. Goodnite.

WADE: Gudnite

Jane drifted off to sleep a few minutes later. She could still hear Donna's muffled voice and the one-sided conversation drifting through the bedroom door.

28

The day of the wedding of Donna Jo Sizemore and Evan Randall Tucker, the sky was sunny and the mercury rose fast. Donna, her sister Ann, Jane, Violet, and Pete's girlfriend Tina, sat in the beauty salon all morning to get their hair done. No one really knew Tina, but Jenny had insisted that Donna needed one bridesmaid for every one of Evan's four sons and groomsmen. Tina was a tiny little waif of a thing who seemed intimidated to be in a wedding surrounded by people she didn't know, but seemed nice enough.

The final wedding line up was confusing for everyone. Ann was the maid of honor and Randy was the best man. Therefore, they were walking together, instead of Violet walking with her husband Randy. Evan wanted his boys in age order standing next to him. But Jane had almost been maid of honor and Donna argued, just as important. So she wanted Jane to be in line after Ann. Everyone agreed Jane and Wade should walk together, although that now corrupted the age order of the groomsmen. Jane could only assume the insistence came from a desire by everyone involved in *this* wedding to make Jane and Wade the next couple wed. That left second-oldest Josh to be the third groomsman, walking with his sister-in-law Violet. That left Pete to walk with his girlfriend that no one really knew, Tina.

They went back to Donna's apartment to all do their makeup. They put on their dresses and jewelry. They got in the limo and rode to the church. By then it was so hot that Donna had sweated off all her make up, and it all had to be reapplied. Of course, it didn't help that her nerves caused Donna to not eat any real food all morning. All that was in her stomach were two cans of Red Bull and two rolls of Tums. Even Donna realized how foolish this was, in retrospect.

"Ugh. This wedding the groom might end up wearing the bride's vomit."

Donna was tucked away in a back room of the church in the immediate time prior to the ceremony. Jane had been running out into the sanctuary, checking on decorations and guests. She had only a few minutes to greet Mr. and Mrs. Riley and Miley and Kiley.

When the wedding party had arrived at the church, the grand sun was streaming in from the stained glass windows, making the room appear very bright. As Jane headed back to get Donna to start the wedding, she noticed the sanctuary seemed very dark, even with all the lights on. Jane was scared to look out a regular window and see what was outside. She could already hear rumblings from the guests about "a real storm kicking up outside." Jane hoped that Donna wouldn't notice. She might take it as a bad omen and call off the wedding.

Donna was at the back of the church with the bridesmaids, waiting for their music cue, when the lights flickered.

"Oh my God. There *is* a storm coming. Maybe we should delay the wedding till it blows over," Donna said loud enough that the guests in the back row were looking in their direction.

"You could be right," Ann said.

Jane jumped in.

"Seriously Donna, you should just go ahead with your vows. You could be done by the time the storm hits."

"You sure, Honey?" Donna fretted worriedly. The music changed in the next room.

"Yes! Oh, Tina, that's your cue."

Tina intertwined arms with Pete and they began down the aisle. Next were Violet and Josh. Jane took Wade's arm and followed them down the aisle.

"How goes it?" Wade leaned slightly to whisper in her ear. A photographer suddenly popped up in front of them, snapping pictures at a mile a minute and preserving their awkward expressions for all eternity.

"Donna is freaking." Jane hoped her short reply conveyed the long list of things that she could not articulate at this particular time.

"Dad, too," Wade said, never breaking his smile. They were almost to the altar.

"Really?" Jane replied, a little too loudly to pretend they weren't having a conversation.

Wade bugged out his sky blue eyes and nodded. They separated, Jane going to the left, Wade to the right. Jane watched Ann and Randy make their way down the aisle. Jane looked at all the bridesmaids lined up in their orange dresses, holding their bouquets of tiger and white lilies. The florist deserved an extra big tip for keeping the flowers from wilting in the heat. They looked like royal handmaidens waiting to receive a queen. When the music changed to the familiar wedding march, Donna came into view. Her dress really was beautiful, all ivory. It was simple enough for a second wedding of a mature woman. It also had enough lace and beads to achieve her unfulfilled dreams from her first wedding. Jane willed Donna not to trip on her dress as she made her way down the aisle.

The guests were all doing their best to focus on the bride and not the wind that was gusting loudly outside. Jane breathed a sigh of relief as Donna met Evan at the altar. They both seemed to visibly relax as they took each other's hands. Jane knew they would both be OK now, no matter what. She wiped away a quick tear, just as the first rumble of thunder beat the reverend to his first line. The guests all looked around nervously, as if they suddenly had developed the ability to see through stained glass and walls. Then they quickly plastered the smiles back onto their faces. Donna seemed to squeeze Evan's hand a little tighter.

The minister began the service. If everyone else was anxious to get the ceremony over with, he certainly was not. He spoke using the same even, slow cadence that Jane suspected he used every Sunday. She shared a look with Wade. He rolled his eyes at her and she giggled. The damn photographer took her picture at that moment. This made Wade laugh. He tried to hide it, but Randy noticed and elbowed him in the ribs. Leave it to the Tucker boys to not even know how to settle down in a wedding ceremony.

The lights flickered a few more times. Then the lightning made it hard to distinguish just what was flashing. Just as Evan kissed the bride, loud rain started to pour down on the roof of the church. It echoed around the open space in the room. If it had started sooner, no one would have been able to hear the vows. Then the town's tornado siren sounded. Everyone was up in a flash and headed down to the church's basement. Luckily, it was large enough for all the wedding guests to fit. The photographer chased after them, furiously snapping the chaos.

"Are you both OK?" Jane asked Donna and Evan, who were still standing at the altar.

"Oh yes, you two go ahead, we are going to, uh, go down the back way," Donna said, a look in her eyes that Jane didn't recognize.

"C'mon," Wade towed her away from them with a smile on his face.

"We should go back. I'm really worried about her."

"I wouldn't be," Wade smiled.

Jane had to take her medium-heeled dress shoes off to make it down the stairs. Her feet were already killing her. The shoes also seemed to be turning her feet orange.

In the basement, people had begun folding up tables from Wednesday night potlucks so that there would be more standing room. About this time, the power went out. It was pitch black in the basement, except for a couple people who had lighters. There were plenty of candles upstairs, but no one wanted to go up to retrieve them and chance getting blown away. Someone turned on a flashlight on their cell phone. The storm raged on outside. Jane and Wade couldn't even find their immediate family members in the room, although she knew they had all headed down here.

"I didn't see Donna come down. Where could they be?" Jane said, as Wade pulled her closer to him.

"I bet they are starting their honeymoon early."

"Oh, no way! That is your dad you are talking about!"

"If it was our wedding day, that is what I would want to do."

"And you think about that a lot, do you? Our wedding day?" Jane accused Wade.

"Well, no. But I do think about having sex with you a lot."

"Shhh. We are in a church. You don't want God to strike you down, do you?"

Then they all heard it. A big roar that seemed to move around the church, like a hungry dinosaur. Jane buried her head into Wade's chest and whimpered. They braced for some sort of impact. Wade wrapped himself around Jane as best he could. There were audible gasps in the room as glass began to break upstairs.

"The windows," a woman cried.

"I love you, Wade," Jane's voice was no more than a whisper among the groans of the building around them.

"I love you, Janie Riley. Always have, always will."

And Jane suddenly had no more air in her lungs. She could only manage short, shallow breaths. What if this was it? This could be the end of her short life. She hadn't even had time to replay it in her head. She hadn't even gotten to sort out the good parts from the bad. She surely had more to say to Wade. Her family, she had to find them. She had to tell them she loved them, too. And Donna and Mr. Tucker. Their life together was just starting. This couldn't be the end of everything, could it? That would make this the worst reality show of her life ever. Jane felt light-headed from the lack of oxygen. She clung to Wade tighter.

Just as fast as it had come, the loud roar faded away. A few of the men, including the minister and the mayor, pushed through the crowd. They went upstairs to check the damage and see if the immediate threat was over. Soon others moved upstairs as well. Everyone could hear now that the storm was clearly moving away from them. Jane stayed right where she was until Wade began to move toward the stairs. He led her up. Indeed, many of the windows had been damaged, but the rest of the church seemed intact. As they headed out the front door, they found the happy couple, safe and sound.

And glowing?

A sort of unofficial receiving line had formed. People were giving much quicker well-wishes than usual, as they hurried to survey the damage of the rest of the town.

"Oh God, there you are! I was so worried." Jane crushed Donna in a big hug. Then she gave one to Mr. Tucker as well.

"I'm so sorry. I told you to go ahead with the wedding. But we could have all been flattened in the church because of me!"

"Oh, it was fine. We would have stopped the ceremony if the siren had gone off sooner. And the church is still standing. You shouldn't have worried about us. We were spending some quality time together. I wasn't going to let some old tornado stop me from consummating my marriage," Donna said emphatically.

"Oh, uh. TMI!" Jane yelled.

"I told you," Wade said knowingly.

"T-M-What?" Donna asked.   But Jane had spotted her family in the parking lot, and rushed over to see if they were all alright.   Wade headed off in the direction of his brothers.

29

No one at the church had been injured. A few cars in the parking lot were damaged. The wedding guests moved on to the reception, figuring it was the best place to gather anew. Some went to check on family members or neighbors first.

The tornado had missed most of the town. It had totally destroyed the Diner. This made Jane sad. The Diner had been the first place in town where she had started to come out of her shell. She had been required to socialize there. She was paid to. The regulars there had stopped thinking of her as that "shy" Riley girl. But Mr. Farley, the owner, swore he would rebuild. It seemed Mr. Tucker might not have such a hard time getting Donna to take time off from work after all.

Some houses sustained moderate damage. Mr. Tucker lost one of his aluminum grain storage bins and an outbuilding. Actually, the outbuilding had landed on the grain storage bin. He wasn't even upset. He told everyone it could have been so much worse. He was covered by insurance. Donna and Evan had to check on that before arriving at the reception. They didn't make a grand entrance as newlyweds usually would, but instead spent their time visiting with everyone at the tables and gathering news.

The afternoon began to get late, so the buffet was set up. People grabbed some food at their convenience. The Tuckers were not the first to eat. Jane didn't realize how hungry she was until she got light-headed. Wade forced her to sit down and eat. Even people not invited to the reception were stopping in for a bite and an update. No one minded. Mr. Tucker had always been generous to the whole town. Poor Jenny did look visibly distraught. She could never have planned for all this.

Then the fire chief, who was also a close personal friend of Mr. Tucker's, came to inform everyone that while there were a handful of minor injuries and destroyed property, there were no casualties in Oakley from the tornado.

"Now that's a reason to throw a party!" Donna had declared. With that, the DJ skipped all the first dance nonsense and cranked up the tunes.

With the excitement over, Jane started to relax. She went to sit with her family. Mr. and Mrs. Riley sat at the same table, putting the twins very obviously between them. They both told her how beautiful she looked in the ceremony and how much they missed her. Miley and Kiley were psyched to be back in their hometown. Many of their old friends were at the reception too. Jane updated everyone about what classes she was taking. They seemed surprised at her sudden interest in agriculture, but Jane didn't want to get into the details.

Tonight she could forgive her parents for everything. She was just so happy that everyone she cared about had come through the tornado without a scratch. Well, except where she had scratched Wade, out of fear. While Jane missed the illusion of family she had had while living in Oakley in their old house, she knew she was happier on her own. She was already closer to her sisters than she had ever been when they lived under the same roof. She could thank modern technology for that.

Mr. and Mrs. Riley had apparently been dealing with their own issues back then. Too bad they hadn't been able to let their children know. They probably thought that it was better to try to hide their difficulties. They were that type of people. But everyone who lived in that house had suffered because of it.

Miley wandered off with her friends, and Kiley took up a keen interest in the DJ. Feeling parched from all the talking, Jane went up to the bar to get another Coke. Evan was up there, getting one more beer. He gave Jane another hug. It felt very natural. She had never seen Mr. Tucker in such high spirits. Usually he was all business.

Out of her peripheral vision, Jane caught sight of a red-headed woman glaring at her from the other end of the bar. The woman looked at her as if Jane had just backed over her dog with a car. When Jane turned, Evan did too. Jane was startled that anyone would be in a bad mood at this party. The surprised look on Jane's face was then reflected on Evan's. The woman quickly advanced on them, leaving no time to think of proper or tactful things to say, for any of them.

"You invited her? I can't believe you invited her! And put her *in* the wedding!" The woman's face was distorted with hate. She might as well have been spitting venom.

Jane realized she recognized this woman. She had been the rude woman at the mall who had collided with her when she was with Miley and Kiley.

"Connie. Please. Jane is Donna's dear friend. And mine."

Oh. Connie Leigh Tucker. So this woman had very good reason not to like Jane. She had disliked her since before she was born. Of all the bad ways Jane had pictured that she might meet her birth mother someday, this was worse.

"I can't believe you would bring my past here to rub my face in it," Connie snarled, seemingly not hearing the reasons Mr. Tucker had just given her.

"Connie, no one knows anything about it except the three of us. It's my intention to keep it that way," Evan said in his best calm, yet authoritative voice. It was probably the tone he used on Wade while he was growing up. There was a little bit of drunkenness mixed with 'don't ruin my wedding day' attitude. It was the only hint of evidence Jane had ever seen that Evan could be nasty to someone if the situation called for it.

Connie turned and looked directly into Jane's eyes.

"Why did you have to go and poke your nose into my past?"

"It is my past, too." It came out of Jane's brain automatically. She didn't stop to think Connie would take it as a smart-mouthed comeback. Jane stated it as the fact that it was. With that, Connie turned and marched back to her table. Mr. Tucker and Jane just stood there at the bar, holding their drinks. They watched her say something to two teenagers at a table across the room, who practically jumped out of their seats for what must have been a command. They grabbed their purses and party favors, and headed out the door.

"I'm so sorry, Jane," Mr. Tucker said, sounding tired all of a sudden. "That would be, I guess, your half-brother and sister. Connie really is the rudest relative that I think I have. I wish you had been born to any other person in my family. Even me. I already think of you as a daughter."

Jane smiled. "That's funny, because Donna and I are on the cusp of a mother/daughter relationship ourselves."

"Well, it sounds to me like you have fashioned yourself a fine family, Janie Riley. If you don't like the family you have, get a new one."

"What are you two roosters crowing about over here?" Donna let go of her dress that she had been lifting as she walked. It made a loud swish. She gave a skeptical look to both of them that said she had caught the whole Connie confrontation.

"Oh, we were just talking about how you and I are like a mother and father to Jane here," Evan said.

"Well, Jane, don't let that stop you from marrying our son Wade someday. We can seat all the guests on the same side of the church if we have to," Donna added.

"Alright." Jane began to cry a little.

"Honey, your adopted parents might have chosen you, and that hasn't seemed to work out real well for you. But you chose us as, well, parental figures and friends, and from my view, it seems like that has worked out a lot better for you," Donna spoke in a motherly tone that Jane was not even aware that she had in her. Jane dove toward them to hug them both. They hugged her back.

"Congratulations, you guys. I hope it's forever." Then Jane turned away quickly, back toward the tables. She had to find Wade. She wiped the tears out of her eyes with her index fingers.

30

The music thumped through the reception hall. Jane and Wade could hear the bass where they were, but could not make out the words to the songs. They were in the room where Donna and Mr. Tucker had stashed their clothes to change into at the end of the night. They sat in the dark room on the small fainting couch. The only light came in from the hallway under the door. Jane couldn't believe that Donna was still wearing her bulky wedding dress. But Donna said she paid so much for it and it was the only day it would be in fashion, so she was going to wear it for as long as possible.

Wade massaged the inside of Jane's mouth with his tongue. He ran a hand through her hair, that had already been released from its restrictive updo. She unbuttoned his dress shirt and slid it off his shoulders. Wade unbuttoned the cuffs so that he could remove it. Then she pulled the plain white T-shirt he wore under it off over his head. Even in the dim light, she could tell it had mussed up his hair that he was wearing longer than usual. She ran her hands across his nearly smooth chest. The combination got her blood pumping. She played with the few blond hairs at the center. She put her lips on his neck and sucked up to his ear and back down to just under the line of his chin to his Adam's apple. He let out a small moan.

"Oh, how I've missed you and the things you do to me."

Jane giggled a low, sex-hungry giggle. She had been in town for four days and had not had one second alone with Wade. She hadn't seen him for a month before that. Her need to be with him was growing more intense by the minute. And having to look at him all day in his tuxedo, well, it didn't help matters.

"Slow down there, girl. If this is how you react when you almost get killed by a tornado, I am going to have to arrange for that to happen more often," Wade drawled.

"It wasn't the tornado. I mean, that wasn't all of it. I met my real mom tonight."

"Oh my God, I'm sorry. She's—someone should have warned you about her." To be correct, four, make that five, people knew that Jane was Connie's daughter.

"Yes, she was very— But I learned tonight that I have a great set of fake parents I can rely on. Ones I adopted myself."

"So, let me get this straight. We are kissing second cousins by blood. And now you think of my father and my step-mother as your own parents? Wow, that's fucked up."

"Oh, I think they are OK with it."

Just then the bass of the music died down and voices could be heard through the speaker system. Some of the sound was muffled where Jane and Wade sat, but they could make out enough to get the gist of what was happening in their absence.

"I know we are running late

Thank you ------------------------- special day

Let's gather around------throwing of the bouquet

And garter-----------

Gather round, gather-----------

Is everyone here?

I'm told we are waiting for -------

Wade and Jane

Anybody know where they are?"

"Ya, I think you're right," Wade said. They both laughed. Then their lips met again. Wade wrapped his arms around her and slowly unzipped her dress. She stood up and he slipped it off her to the floor. He removed her strapless bra while she undid his belt and let his pants hit the floor. He sucked on one nipple, and then the other. Jane moaned softly.

"You better be quick. It sounds like things are wrapping up out there," Jane said breathlessly.

Wade picked her up and threw her down on the small couch.

"Usually women don't ask me to be quick," he wisecracked.

And he kissed her deeply.

EPILOGUE

Years later, Jane would talk to Miley and Kiley about the home environment they grew up in. Jane wasn't the only one to feel left out. It had nothing to do with her being adopted. M & K felt like they didn't receive enough parental love and attention as well. That was why they worked so hard in sports, to seek attention that way. Their parents' marriage had suffered for longer than any of them had suspected, and taken its toll on everyone.

After high school, Kiley went off to college, studying English. Miley tried her hand at several jobs, trying to find something that fit her personality.

Connie stopped talking to Evan Tucker's family.

"She must *really* not like me," Jane had told Mr. Tucker, who now insisted that she call him Evan.

"She doesn't like me or my kids anymore. No skin off my nose," he said, trying to soften the blow for Jane. He had kept his word and paid for Jane's higher education. She, in turn, kept her promise to him.

Jane moved back to Oakley, the only town she had ever known, except for her three and a half years in Burkeville attending college. She stayed in Wade's apartment. "Their apartment" now. They always talked about how it was too small and they should rent a little house where they could have more room and a dog. But they spent so much time at Evan's house, that at the end of the day, it just seemed unnecessary.

Jane was busier than usual in the Tucker Farms office when Pete called on a chilly spring morning. Sick of the unusually cold winter, Evan and Donna were away on a trip to Hawaii. Jane was working on the billing and invoices. They were not a part of her regular, day-to-day job, because Evan usually liked to handle them himself. Evan was very good at math. Plus, he said that way if there was a dispute later, he would have no one else to blame but himself. But someone had to fill in for him while he was gone.

"Pete to Jane." The walkie-talkie squawked to life on the desk. Everyone on the farm just called it a radio. For Jane, using it was one of the funnest parts of working on the farm.

"Go," Jane responded.

"Hurry, you got to come out here. There is something wrong with the ventilation equipment in elevator twelve." Pete sounded weird on the other end.

"How do you know?" Jane was skeptical.

"Because it isn't on— Ya, it lost power."

"Did you try hitting it?" Usually one part of the system would quit working, not whole damn thing.

"Oh ya, 50 times. You better come check it out."

"Copy," Jane replied.

Jane threw on her jacket and headed outside. It seemed like there was always something gone afoul to keep them all busy. Jane was halfway out to the grain silos in the farm's utility vehicle, essentially a golf cart on steroids, when she realized something was out of place. Someone had vandalized one of the silos. Jane started to sweat. Evan would be furious about this.

How had she not noticed when she had gone into the office this morning? Unless someone had done it afterwards.

But how would someone get away with that without one of the brothers noticing?

Who would do such a thing?

Then, she read what it said. She stopped the cart so hard that she almost ejected herself from it right over the engine.

In giant red letters, the silo said:

MARRY ME JANE? ♥WADE

Oh my God. They had been going out for four years. They had talked about marriage here and there, as part of some distant future. But now the future was today. Jane didn't know how long she sat there staring at the giant words meant for her. Eventually she became aware that Wade's pick-up was approaching her. He pulled up next to her and stopped, the brakes squealing in protest, a small cloud of dirt from his tires whooshed past them both. They looked at each other.

"So?" Wade asked.

"Yes," Jane said, as she jumped out of the cart and attempted to hug Wade through the wide open window of his truck. The hug turned into passionate kisses. Wade eventually just pulled her through the window and onto his lap.

"Was that too corny for you?" Wade asked. Jane could tell there was genuine worry behind his joke.

"Nope. Just the right amount of corn for me."

In a sequel to *The Wind Could Blow a Bug*—

Kiley Riley has no idea that she is about to find inspiration for her next book through a hot affair when she returns to her small hometown in Alabama. After graduating college and going on tour to promote her first book, Kiley thinks she is just returning home to celebrate the holidays and become an aunt. But staying in the same house with her pregnant sister Jane, Jane's husband, and all his attractive farm boy brothers is full of surprises. Kiley discovers that you find love *When You Least Expect It*…

WHEN YOU LEAST EXPECT IT

COMING IN 2015

JENNIFER FRIESS lives in Lenawee County, Michigan, with her husband, son, and two dogs. She loves entertainment trivia. She doesn't match her socks. She is a picky eater and likes it that way. Jennifer has written several unpublished short stories. *The Wind Could Blow a Bug* is her first published novel.

Follow Jennifer here:

BLOG: ImNotStalkingYou.com
My mildly entertaining random thoughts

TWITTER: @jenf2

FACEBOOK: www.facebook.com/imnotstalkingyou2

www.ingramcontent.com/pod-product-compliance
Lightning Source LLC
Chambersburg PA
CBHW050937120626
46552CB00001B/245